The

Judas

Kiss

The Judas Kiss

The Tyburn Trilogy, Book III

Maggie MacKeever

Vintage Ink Press

Maggie MacKeever
Visit my website at www.maggiemackeever.com

Printed in the United States of America

First Printing: Oct 2018
Vintage Ink Press

ISBN-978-0-9895197-0-0

For Lee. Always.

Prologue

Then came Corinna in a long loose gown… — Ovid

A heavy traveling carriage, drawn by four horses, rattled along the Great Dover Road. Inside, a mahogany-haired young Englishwoman was attempting to read Apuleius's *Metamorphises* in the original Latin, no minor feat in light of the jolting of the coach, while her companion, a plump dark-haired senhora of some thirty-odd years, murmured soothing nonsense to the wicker basket in her lap. That the occupant of the basket greatly disliked traveling had become apparent during the long journey from Portugal.

"Patience, *piquero*," crooned the senhora. "It will not be much longer now."

Lady Clea Marsden, *née* Fairchild — the 'lady' courtesy of her brother, who'd petitioned for the privilege; if he must be burdened with a title, Ned had declared, his sister might as well enjoy whatever benefit their unexpected change in status might confer — glanced out the carriage window. "We are not far from London. Shooter's Hill is one of the highest points around. If you care to look, you may see Severndroog Castle, built to commemorate Commodore Sir William James, who attacked and destroyed a pirate fortress at Suvarnadurg along the western coast of India."

The senhora did *not* care to look, that lady announced; she was quite comfortable where she was. Or if not precisely *comfortable*, she amended, at least she had achieved a tolerable compromise between the unwelcoming coach seat and her aching bones.

Clea sank back on her own uncomfortable seat. "Shooter's Hill was once a favorite haunt of highwaymen. But you needn't worry. Highwaymen are no longer as common as crows."

Even as she spoke there came shouts from outside. Horses snorted. The coach jolted to a halt.

The senhora rolled her eyes. "What now?" she sighed.

Abruptly, the door was wrenched ajar. In the opening loomed a brigand wearing a neckcloth tied around his face with holes cut out for his eyes. In one hand he brandished a businesslike blunderbuss.

Age? thought Clea. *Young. Stature? Sturdily built. Hair almost as black as Pilar's own.* She slipped her fingers under the brim of the brown silk bonnet resting beside her on the seat.

"Stand and deliver!" the highwayman demanded. Clea added, silently, *Voice rough and disguised.*

The senhora clutched the wicker basket to her ample bosom. "Why should I stand? And deliver what? You English are all mad."

Outside, the coachman was objecting. A rough voice told him to hold his whid. Clea said, "This ruffian means to rob us, Pilar."

The highwayman snarled at her. Clea pulled a large flintlock pistol from underneath her bonnet and fired. He tumbled back and out of sight.

Men shouted, horses squealed, the coach lurched. Gasped the senhora, "*Santo Deus!* Is he dead?"

"Hardly. I merely shot him in the shoulder." Clea peered out through the open door. As the highwayman heaved himself onto his horse, his companion — shorter, stockier, also masked — wheeled his mount. The marauders set off riding at breakneck speed down the roadway. Clea ordered the coachman to drive on, closed the door and resumed her seat.

The carriage lumbered forward. Pilar settled the basket more securely on her lap. "That makes four villains you have vanquished. Or is it five? We Portuguese have a saying. *A curiosidade matou o gato.* Curiosity killed the cat."

In its wicker basket, her own cat muttered.

Clea took refuge in her book.

Meanwhile, some distance down that same road, another conversation was taking place.

"You didn't say we was to snaffle a gentry mort," complained Ingler Charlie, thusly called result of his primary occupation being a horse dealer of shady character. "*Or* that she'd have about her person a barking iron. To my way of thinking, it serves you right as you got winged."

His companion pointed the blunderbuss in his direction. "Stop blubbering."

Charlie wasn't blubbering but complaining, he protested, and who had a better right? This snaffling of a gentry mort wasn't what he had agreed to, not that anything specific had been agreed to, nor would it have been had he been given the word with no bark on it, because at the first mention of snaffling Charlie would have hedged off. In fact, he meant to hedge off now, just as soon as Toby left off bleeding like a stuck pig; whatever one might say about Ingler Charlie — Charlie was aware that much was said about him, most of it uncomplimentary — he wasn't one to leave a fellow in dire straits, not that they was sailors, or on a ship, or anywhere near a sea ...

In any event, it queered him why anyone would want to make off with a gentry mort, especially one so unobliging as this particular gentry mort had shown herself to be.

Toby's finger tightened on the trigger. "It weren't my idea."

Then whose idea was it, Charlie would like to know. Or maybe he would not. He finished binding Toby's neckcloth around his shoulder; pulled his own neckcloth off his face and fashioned a sling. The men had taken refuge in a clearing, some distance from where the attempted snaffling had taken place.

Toby rose unsteadily to his feet. Charlie heaved himself upright with some difficulty, horse dealers of bad character not often having cause to go lolling about on the ground. "If we was meant to snatch her," he added, as he brushed himself off, "why'd you ask for her purse? You could have snatched both her *and* her purse and no one the wiser, if not—"

"Stow it!" Toby was staring over Charlie's shoulder, his face gone white.

Someone had stole up behind him, Charlie realized. Someone who was holding a sharp-bladed frumper tight against his throat.

"It weren't our fault," Toby whined.

"It never is your fault," the holder of the knife said icily. "Why have you brought a crackbrain into the business? A beak need only look crosswise at him and he'll squeak beef."

Crackbrain Charlie might be, but he didn't fail to recognize that voice. Could he have gazed upon the owner of the knife, not that he cared to do so thank you very much, he would have seen a fair-haired man dressed almost all in churchly black.

A costume which, as Charlie understood it, though his understanding admittedly was far from perfect, nicely demonstrated the principle of irony.

If only Toby hadn't invited him to engage in a spot of business. If only Charlie hadn't assumed Toby meant the sort of business generally embarked upon by knights of the road.

If only he'd said no to Toby, he might be safe at home in bed with the covers tucked up to his chin.

But he hadn't, had he? And now the Deacon was holding a knife at his throat.

Sweat trickled down Charlie's temples, dripped onto his cheek. "And what have you to say about all this?" the Deacon murmured in his ear.

"M-mum's the word!" Charlie stammered. "I'll take tippin with the devil afore a word of this day's doings slips past me lips."

"In the midst of life, we are in death," the Deacon murmured.

Charlie screamed as the sharp blade bit into his flesh.

Chapter One

It is a great thing to know one's vices. — Cicero

Baron Saxe was enjoying a splendidly erotic dream. Silk stockings were involved, plain with laced clocks. A blue ribbon garter. An exquisitely turned ankle, an elegant calf.

He slid his hand up the smooth length of the lady's leg. Leaned forward to press his mouth against the sweet flesh of her knee. Inhaled the rich mingled scents of frangipani, heliotrope, musk.

"Such resilience, my lord," drawled an amused voice. "And after last night. I am impressed."

He was caressing not a hitherto-unexplored knee, Kane realized, but a familiar wrist. He gave it one last salute and rolled over on his back. The sudden movement made his head swim.

Gingerly, he opened one eye. Bright light streamed through tall windows draped with blue damask that matched the hangings of the huge domed tester bed where he sprawled on silken sheets. The wallpaper boasted a similar stripe. Satinwood toilet-table with folding top; massive wardrobe and welcoming wing chairs; a number of cleverly placed mirrors and advantageously situated wall sconces and oil lamps—

A woman was standing by the bed. "Drink this." She held out a glass.

With difficulty, Kane levered himself up on one elbow, took the glass, choked down its vile contents. "Thank you, Lilah," he muttered, and sank back on the sheets.

"I warned you about the absinthe," she said. "If you will recall. Or probably you don't recall, but I promise you I did."

What was it she'd told him? Kane captured a wisp of memory. Absinthe enlivened the spirit, cured hepatitis and fistulas and gout.

A pity absinthe wasn't equally efficacious regarding the exercise of common sense.

Images of the previous evening flashed in front of his eyes. All work and no play, Lilah had informed him, made Jack very humdrum company. Consequently, Jack — or in this case Kane — had found himself exploring the nuances of various amatory contortions described in the *Kama Sutra*: the Congress of a Dog, a Goat, a Deer; the Pressing of an Elephant, the Rubbing of a Boar, the Jumping of a Tiger, and the Mounting of an Ass.

He had, in short, proved himself quite venturesome, the result of which was chafing in certain portions of his anatomy and a pounding in his head.

Kane eyed his companion. Lilah Kingston bore little resemblance to the popular perception of a bawdy house abbess. A modest high-necked dove-grey gown covered her supple body from shoulder to wrist, neck to toe. Her thick chestnut hair lay coiled simply at her nape. She was neither blowsy nor buxom, powdered or rouged.

A smile lurked in the depths of her lavender eyes. "I will leave you to recuperate, my lord. Join me when you are more the thing." Quietly, she left the room.

Kane doubted he would ever be more the thing. His head felt as if a dozen demons were drumming on it, his mouth tasted like camel dung.

Much as he might like to, Kane could not spend the day abed. He made his way unsteadily to the corner basin stand; stood there several moments before summoning the energy to splash water on his person, shrug on his jacket and breeches, pull on his boots. Marginally refreshed by these exertions, he walked out into the hallway and down the stair.

The Academy was richly appointed, its interior designed in the style of the Adams Brothers, its furnishings inspired by Sheraton and Heppelwhite. Kane encountered no other guests, this most popular of brothels not being open for business at so early an hour.

A liveried footman, young and handsome, waited outside Lilah's private sitting room. As Kane approached, he opened the door.

Door-opening was one of the more conventional duties a handsome young hireling might be required to perform in this house.

The sitting room was small but elegantly appointed with rosewood furniture and expensive Argand lamps and silk paper on the walls. Above the fireplace hung a large oil painting: Lilah, magnificently nude by firelight.

When a man enjoys two women at the same time, and equally, it is called the United Congress. When a man enjoys many women together, it is called the Congress of a Herd of Cows.

She poured him a cup of coffee. Kane sat down beside her on the brocaded loveseat.

Lilah picked up *The Times*, which she had been reading. " 'It is not from any scandal to herself, nor from detriment to public morals, that the Queen-Consort of England can be prosecuted as a traitor under English law, but because she may give a spurious heir to the Crown and plunge the monarchy into civil commotion.' " She lowered the paper. "The threat hardly seems imminent, Caroline being past her child-bearing years."

Kane could not escape the current Royal debacle even in a house of prostitution, he thought gloomily. All the world was avidly observing the Prince and Princess of Wales, who for many years had existed in a state of mutual antipathy, and were currently engaged in outright war.

Upon the death of his father in January, Prinny had immediately begun devising schemes to divorce his detested wife and prevent her from being crowned on the basis of her highly improper relationship with one Bartolomeo Pergami, sixteen years her junior, who had progressed in her employ from courtier to chamberlain to, allegedly, bedmate. The resultant Bill of Pains and Penalties was in effect a trial by act of Parliament: Caroline would be declared innocent or guilty according to a simple majority of votes. Unfortunately, the King had failed to anticipate that his determination to unseat his Queen would bring her home for the first time since she departed England six years earlier. Nor had he foreseen that a great many Londoners would flock to champion his lady, which had less to do with Her Majesty than with how much he himself was disliked.

"To be consistent with the wording of the Bill," Kane said, "the Queen's acts must have amounted to 'gross, scandalous and licentious conduct' that has brought dishonor to the country and threatened the dignity of the Crown. And if that isn't a case of the gander and the goose, I don't know what is."

Lilah was regarding him, her expression sympathetic. Kane added, "I am poor company, I fear."

"You are excellent company." She reached for the coffee pot and refilled his cup. "As several of the girls remarked last night."

Kane immediately recalled an additional exertion, this one involving the Standing Wheelbarrow and a female whose face he could not recall. To distract himself, and his companion, he inquired about her latest business venture, the Temple of Beauty in Bond Street, where she dispensed patent medicines, ointments and unguents and emulsions to females eager to stave off the ravages of aging and decay.

Which was admittedly a step above the peddling of human flesh.

"The response has been gratifying," Lilah told him, with more enthusiasm than was her custom. "Our Magnetic Rock Dew Water for removing wrinkles and restoring color to grey hair is second in popularity only to our exclusive Jordan water, which is delivered direct from the legendary river itself, you understand."

"My felicitations." More likely, her exclusive water was delivered direct from the Thames.

A scratch came at the door. The young footman entered. "Mr. Pritchett requests a word with Baron Saxe."

Lilah arched an eyebrow. "A Bow Street Runner on our doorstep? I trust you didn't leave him standing in the street."

The footman backed hastily out of the room. Kane said, "Before you ask, I don't know why Pritchett's here. For that matter, I don't know how he knew *I* was here."

"You visiting so seldom? That horse won't run, my dear." Lilah folded her newspaper neatly and set it aside.

Before Kane could become involved in a discussion of how often he was or was not to be found at the Academy, the footman returned with a neat little man wearing a dark coat and trousers, white linen, plaid vest, carefully shined shoes. On the Runner's nose rested wire-rimmed spectacles. Under one arm was tucked a gilt-topped baton. In his hands he held a bowl-shaped hat.

"How kind of you to grace my humble establishment with your presence, Mr. Pritchett," Lilah remarked ironically. "May I provide you with tea, coffee, chocolate? No? Perhaps a whore?"

The Runner's fingers tightened on his hat brim. "I thank you kindly, ma'am, but no."

"Then I will leave you to it, gentlemen." Lilah closed the door behind her with a distinctly displeased thunk.

Kane winced. "Well, man? What is so urgent that it brings you here?"

Pritchett's eyes drifted to the nude painting above the fireplace. He jerked them away. "I wouldn't have interrupted, my lord, but I reckoned you'd want to be informed."

Kane repeated, irritably, "Informed of *what*?"

The Runner shifted his slight weight from one foot to the other. "Clea Fairchild has come home."

Chapter Two

Nothing has more strength than dire necessity. —
Euripides

"Me, I do not enjoy this London." Senhora Estevez frowned at a mullioned library window through which seeped dreary grey light. "It is just like you English to hide away the sun."

Clea looked up from the note she was penning. A blaze of color in a poppy red morning gown, Pilar more than compensated for the dullness of the day. Atop her dark hair the senhora wore an absurd lace cap, liberally festooned with cheerful ribbons, which she proclaimed befit her status as a matron of some thirty years. Artistically draped about her voluptuous poppy-red person was a brilliant Kashmir shawl.

"We English are a disobliging lot," Clea admitted. "Shall I have a fire built?"

The senhora tsk'd at her. "Not so long ago, if you wanted a fire, you lit it yourself."

Not so long ago Clea had done many things for herself, unlike Pilar, who was as indolent as the cat curled up on her lap, a large muscular creature with sturdy limbs and golden eyes and a thick blue-grey coat. Due to some odd quirk of breeding, Fausto seemed often to be smiling, giving a highly erroneous impression that he was of an amiable temperament.

The cat was not smiling at the moment, but snoring. His paws twitched as if he was crossing continents in his sleep.

Pilar stroked his back. "Compose yourself, sweeting. We will repose ourselves for a time at this house where there are so many fine mouses to eat."

Clea glanced around the drafty chamber. Rodents there were aplenty in this half-timbered Tudor structure perched near the river on the north side of the Thames.

In this particular moment, there were no mouses in sight. Doubtless they were huddled in their nests attempting to keep warm.

Heavy oak furniture adorned with intricately carved animals and flowers was scattered willy-nilly around the large room. Massive molded ceiling beams supported lesser timbers, the spaces between filled with plastered lath. A Bacchanalian chimneypiece featured nubile maidens and satyrs. Stacks of books lined the old shelves, rested tipsily on the floor alongside maps of the world, a calculating board with counters, and a perpetual almanac in a frame. On one corner of the desk sat an amazingly unattractive statue with the head of a hippopotamus, legs of a lion, tail of a crocodile, swollen belly and human breasts.

Clea's brother had spent a great deal of money in an attempt to prevent the ancestral home of their grandmother's family from tumbling down around their ears. This room — for sentimental reasons, Ned professed — he had left largely untouched. It was Clea's favorite refuge. Unlike herself, the library had not changed.

"You have no more conversation today than that ugly statue," Pilar observed. "Fortunately, I am content talking to the cat. Fausto, are you aware that thus far four *vilões* have attempted to accost our friend? Before the intruder at the inn—"

"Whom *you* hit over the head with a chamberpot," Clea pointed out. "Granted, it was no more than he deserved for interrupting you at your ablutions."

"—there was the female who provoked her in the Chiado fruit market. In hindsight I have grown convinced that one had more than purse-snatching in mind. The man on shipboard she shoved into the sea. And now this highwayman. In my country we have a saying: *Homem apercebido, meio combatido.* Forewarned is forearmed."

Clea was put in mind of another Portuguese saying: 'Words are made of silver, but silence is made of gold.' Because Pilar was her dearest friend, she kept the reflection to herself.

Wakely Court's long-suffering butler, a portly individual of middle years clad in somber livery, appeared in the doorway. "The Dowager Countess of Dorset," Tidcombe announced.

Hannah, here so soon? Clea was tempted to duck into one of the many not-so-secret passages that riddled Wakely Court. Instead, she said, "Show her in." With a despairing glance around the untidy room, Tidcombe withdrew.

Clea pushed back her chair and rose, tugged her sleeves into place, twitched the skirt of her pale muslin dress. Pilar asked, with idle interest, "She is a dragon, this dowager?"

"Worse. Cousin Hannah is a stickler for the proper way of doing things." Clea smoothed her rebellious curls.

A small spare woman swathed in black swept into the library, the plumage on her bonnet startlingly reminiscent of the tail feathers of a crow. "Really, Clea! Why am I left to read in the gossip sheets that you have come home? And what is this I hear about you shooting highwaymen? It is dreadfully cold in here! Why haven't you had the fire lit?" She frowned at the library's remaining occupant, who had comfortably arranged herself amidst a plethora of pillows on a fancifully conceived antique chair. "This must be the female you brought with you from Portugal."

"It's nice to see you, too, Cousin Hannah," Clea replied politely. "Permit me to make known to you my friend, Senhora Pilar Estevez. Pilar, this is Lady Dorset, my cousin."

"I am pleased to make your acquaintance, my lady," Pilar murmured, in her native tongue.

Lady Dorset twitched her nose. "What was that she said? This female displays an appalling ignorance of appropriate behavior. I daresay it is because she is a foreigner."

"But no!" Pilar responded, her usual charmingly faint accent suddenly grown as thick as treacle. "It is merely that I do not care to disarrange Fausto, who has enjoyed a fine dinner in this place where there are so many mouses and is now asleep."

As if to underscore her words, Fausto let out a gentle burp.

Hannah cast the cat a disapproving glance, extricated a handkerchief from somewhere about her person and dusted off a chair.

Clea moved toward the fireplace. "Pilar and I became acquainted in Frenada, the little Portuguese village where Wellington made his winter camp."

"Heathens," the dowager said dismissively. "Clea, I cannot approve of you staying alone in this house. What are you doing? Stop that at once!"

Ignoring her cousin's protests, Clea deftly arranged wood and kindling and struck a flint.

The fire caught. "*Muito obrigada!*" said Pilar. Fausto flicked an ear. The dowager looked as aghast as if she'd seen her cousin tie her garter in a public place.

Clea rose, brushed off her hands. "Your concern is unfounded, Hannah. I am hardly alone. Ned's staff is in residence, and additionally I have Pilar to keep me company. Even were all that not true, I am a grown woman and may do as I please."

"Including servants' work, apparently!" the dowager snapped. "What you are is a marvel of wrong-headedness, but that is nothing new. I hold your brother at fault for dragging you about the Peninsula, instructing you in the use of firearms and heaven knows what else. Well-brought-up young women do not go about shooting people, in case you do not know it. Highwaymen, for heaven's sake!"

"*O que é isto?*" Pilar plucked another piece of marzipan from the plate placed on a nearby table. "I do not understand why you English must make a mountain out of the merest molehill. But then, I am an ignorant *estrangeira*, and what can one expect?"

Clea seated herself again behind the desk. "Cousin Hannah is appalled that I accompanied my brother to war. Such things are not done by well-brought-up young females. She conveniently forgets that, prior to the death of her son, the previous earl, Ned and I were the tiniest twigs on the most distant branch of the family tree."

The dowager muttered, "Would that I could."

Clea ignored the interruption. "Once my brother inherited the title, Hannah did her duty and tried her utmost to make me into a lady. We abandoned the enterprise by mutual consent when we perceived it was in the nature of silk purses and sows' ears. Rather, I thought we had abandoned it. Apparently my cousin doesn't agree. You must try

14

and be less critical of my brother, Hannah. Ned is your sole hope of ensuring the continuance of your precious line of Dorset earls."

Color blossomed in the dowager's cheeks.

"*I* was a well-brought-up young woman," commented Pilar. "Until I met Don Miguel. But that is not a proper subject for polite conversation, eh?"

Portugal. White-domed cathedrals and grand plazas lined with sun-drenched cafes. Pastel-color houses decked with laundry. Narrow tree-lined streets where fado *singers performed.* Clea recalled her first glimpse of Don Miguel Sanchez, one of the *guerrilha* chiefs who worked with Wellington. The *bandido* had cut a dashing figure in a pelisse liberated from the 16th Dragoons and an immense hussar cap that had the Eagle of Napoleon reversed, his swarthy features adorned by a marvelous curled moustache of which he'd been exceedingly proud, a brace of pistols tucked into a gaudy red sash.

Don Miguel had kept a mistress in nearly every village, in addition to a wife, all of whom he vowed he would give up for Pilar, who had been extremely annoyed when she discovered he had not.

"Mind your manners, Clea!" Hannah sat up straighter in her chair. "Grown woman or no, you are not so wise as you may believe in the ways of the world. Apropos of which, I have recently had a most enlightening conversation with your mother-in-law. Mariel Marsden told me— I had not realized— This is an appalling business. To lose your husband under such disturbing circumstances—"

"Disturbing circumstances?" Clea echoed. Hannah had no idea. "You make it sound as if I misplaced Harry. I assure you I know exactly where he is."

"If you say such things to Mariel," hissed the dowager, "it's scant surprise she is going about insinuating matters might have turned out differently if you had been a more *appropriate* sort of wife. Don't pull a face at me! I am looking after your best interests. Clearly, someone must." Her irate gaze lit upon the flintlock pistol resting amid the clutter on the desk. "Lud! Is that a *gun?*"

"I keep it close at hand in case I am possessed of a sudden impulse to shoot someone." Since it would hardly be *appropriate* for her to box her cousin's ears, Clea folded her hands in her lap. "You will excuse me if I cut short this conversation, Hannah. I find that I have developed a headache."

The dowager huffed, heaved herself upright, and stalked out of the room.

The door slammed shut behind her. "One should perchance consider this tendency you have to attract ill-wishers," Pilar remarked. Clea unclenched her fingers and reached for her pen.

Chapter Three

A happy life consists in tranquility of mind. — Cicero

Night had descended on the city. Streetlamps cast faint oases of light in the thick fog. Baron Saxe strode through the Doric portico of the Theater Royal in Bow Street and entered the main hall, which was divided into a nave and aisles of three bays.

At the south end of the hall, a short flight of steps led to the grand staircase. The theater boasted a great deal of imitation porphyry, Grecian columns and statuary, by none of which was he impressed.

Twelfth Night had concluded. Kane stopped to speak with none of the several acquaintances who tried to catch his eye. Nor did he engage in any of the conversations going on around him, most of which had to do with the current royal contretemps. Now that the prosecution had finished presenting its case — reported in titillating detail, and with enthusiastic embellishment, by the press — Princess Caroline's lawyers had been granted a brief recess in which to prepare her defense. Thousands of her supporters, laden with addresses, were flocking to the house where she was staying: the inhabitants of the city of Bristol, and of Birmingham; the ladies of Edinburgh; Spitalfields weavers and glassblowers and corsetieres, all wearing white ribbons to proclaim her purity. London was abuzz with talk of spies and secret committees and Green Bags of evidence.

At the head of the staircase, beyond a handsome doorway, lay an anteroom ornamented with yet another marble statue, this one of Shakespeare. On the west side of the anteroom, folding doors opened into a long corridor which provided access to the boxes in the first circle. From the auditorium came muted shouts of "God Save the Queen".

Beyond the south end of the corridor, two staircases linked the three circles of boxes and a central entrance to the lower saloon. The audience was louder here, not only chanting but stamping their feet.

Kane paused in the doorway of Lord Dorset's private box. The current earl and his countess had several months previously withdrawn to their Sussex estate, there to avoid the farce of the Queen's trial and, even more importantly, the machinations of the King's Machiavellian Secretary of State for Foreign Affairs, Lord Castlereagh.

Swathed in her customary black, the Dowager Countess of Dorset was seated at the midpoint of the first row of chairs, much like a spider squatting in the center of its web. Hannah was engaged in animated conversation with her archenemy, Lady Georgiana Ashcroft, a fair antique beauty who was elegant in cobalt silk.

"I am shocked beyond measure by these allegations that Princess Caroline engaged in improper relations with a foreigner of low degree," remarked the dowager. "The Ministers should never have allowed things to come to such a pass."

"Tut!" responded Lady Georgiana. "It is hardly the fault of the Ministers if the Queen dallied where she should not have." Lady Georgiana went on to relate the testimony of two naval officers who had proved evasive about the Princess's sleeping arrangements whilst aboard their sailing vessel; one had, upon being cross-examined, sunk into a swoon. The other officer earnestly explained that Caroline had desired Pergami to sleep in the tent with her due to her fear of being set upon by a pirate ship.

" 'pon rep! Pirates." Color flared in Hannah's sallow cheeks.

Kane had had a sense of humor once. He wondered when it had got lost.

He shut out the ladies' further tittle-tattle. At the opposite side of the box, a slender woman stood surrounded by a group of admiring gentlemen. Mahogany curls piled carelessly atop her head with a ribbon wound through them, an oval face, a straight little nose ... Her tobacco-colored silk muslin gown was the epitome of sophistication, with a high empire-style waistline, shallow round neckline and short puffed sleeves.

Kane had considerable experience with female garments, and their undergarments as well. Definitely, he should not be contemplating what this particular female might or might not be wearing beneath that expensive dress.

Pritchett's information was correct. Clea Fairchild had come home.

Surely it was a trick of the Argand lights, or maybe Kane's tired eyes, that made her seem to glow.

She was not Clea Fairchild but Clea Marsden now, Kane reminded himself; no longer a boyish fifteen-year-old damsel debating whether she should buy false bosoms made of wax. They had last met in Vienna, when the great powers of Europe gathered to settle, amidst feverish gaiety, the future boundaries of the continent. The Congress had been interrupted by Napoleon's escape from Elba, but not before Clea tumbled head over heels in love with one of Wellington's dashing young aides-de-camp.

Two years later, they had married.

A year after that, her handsome lieutenant had been dead.

Clea turned then and saw Kane; extricated herself from her admirers, brushing aside their protests with a laughing remark. As she crossed the box toward him, a renewed chorus of "God Save the Queen" — intermixed, more ominously, with "No Queen, No King" — was drowning out the symphony the orchestra so valiantly attempted to play.

Kane said, when Clea reached his side, "I hear you shot a highwayman."

"Everyone has heard it," she retorted. "I am alternately scolded for my boldness — a lady, Cousin Hannah informs me, should more properly have fainted — and for being a poor shot."

As one of the people responsible for her prowess with a pistol, Kane was tempted to inquire why Clea had chosen merely to disarm. "Ned will be glad to have you back. You remained abroad a long time."

"I am one with Seneca. 'The whole world is my native land'. However, the revolutionary fervor on the Peninsula inspired me finally to come home." Clea studied the unruly audience. "Not that there is any lack of revolutionary fervor here. But you will know about that."

So Kane did. Warnings of revolution reached the Home Office almost daily. Letters were piling up marked 'Plot against Lord Sidmouth', 'Threat to the life of Lord Castlereagh', 'Threat to assassinate the King'.

Clea tucked her hand through Kane's arm. "Are you championing the Queen?"

Kane had also had a sense of purpose once, before exposure to the workings of government had led him to the realization that the world was largely motivated by self-interest, and the further realization that nothing he might do or say would make a whit of difference, human nature being what it was.

And wasn't he in a splendid mood tonight?

"I wouldn't go so far as to say that."

Clea was taller than he remembered. The top of her curly head reached to his chin. Her gown's low neckline afforded a glimpse of breasts that no longer needed assistance from plumpers made of wax.

And lovely breasts they were.

Hastily, Kane averted his gaze.

Those lovely breasts belonged to his friend Ned's little sister, whom he had first dandled on his knee when she was three years old.

Chapter Four

A mouse does not rely on just one hole. — Plautus

Mr. Pritchett of Bow Street made his way through Covent Garden, half-deafened by the shouts of vendors, the clatter of donkeys' and horses' hooves, the rattle of wagon wheels on stone. He passed costermongers selling everything from fruit and vegetables to fried eels, basket women carting heavy loads on their backs and heads, porters jostling for the right of way.

Everywhere he looked, he saw Queenite sentiments scrawled on the sides of buildings and stalls. 'The Queen forever, the King in the river!' 'We will have no King if there is no Queen.'

Many believed that the Queen's case would bring down the Tory administration. Pritchett rather wished it might, not due to any republican principles — Pritchett didn't hold with principles — but because having to choose between several evils was no choice at all.

If Baron Saxe were no longer a man of influence—

But Baron Saxe would always be a man of influence, whether the reins of government were in Tory hands or Whig, and Pritchett was tucked firmly in the baron's pocket, with no hope of escape.

There was a lesson in it. If one was going to stick one's hand into unlawful cookie jars, one should make damned certain not to get caught.

Vegetables and fruits were confined to one section of the piazza, which was bounded on the north and east by arcaded houses. Potatoes and coarser products flourished near the Tuscan portico of St. Paul's Church. Potted flowers and plants bloomed on the west side of the square. In the center were a miscellany of other items from bird-sellers to dealers in old iron to large displays of crockery-ware.

The square stank of unwashed flesh and rotting garbage. Pritchett paused to buy a sprig of lavender from a flower girl. The child trailed at his heels, crying, "Two bundles a penny, primroses! Sweet violets, a penny a bunch!" When he continued to ignore her, she made a graphic suggestion as to what he might do with himself.

Pritchett turned around, prepared to box her ears. She stuck out her tongue and scurried away.

Pritchett raised the lavender to his nose and inhaled.

Bow Street Runners — or thief-takers, as some called them — performed many different tasks, preventative and investigatory and political. Pritchett might attend a costume ball to guard against jewel thieves, or present himself at a bank during shipments of specie; might be called to deal with post office robberies, bank raids, murders, thefts, assaults, swindles or street crimes.

At the moment, he was chasing around the city in pursuit of forged Bank of England certificates, to which end he had spent the past hour listening to the laments of a grocer who had discovered himself to be in the unhappy possession of six forged fifty-pound notes.

False banknotes, queer screens. To do some soft was to pass bad paper money. Flimsies were Bank of England notes.

The fakement of flimsies was a profitable undertaking, the general public being unable to distinguish between good notes and bad. Forgers made the counterfeit notes as dirty as practicable so as to seem they'd been in circulation a long time. As a result, clerks frequently refused payment of genuine notes for fear of being hoodwinked. Even bank officials were often deceived. Pritchett was expected, alongside his other duties, to deliver up the counterfeiters, sooner preferably than later, for which service he would receive a share of the parliamentary rewards given for the seizure and conviction of criminals. Unfortunately, by the time those rewards were split, little would remain.

He shook off these sour reflections. Before him lay his destination. A faded wooden sign portraying three perched pigeons dangled from its eaves. Pritchett fastened the lavender sprig to the lapel of his coat.

Beyond the narrow time-warped doorway, a long covered passage opened into a well-lighted quadrangle and beyond it a long low-ceilinged public room. The air was thick with tobacco smoke. Small lamps glowed in the corners. Sawdust covered the floor.

The proprietor approached, a stout individual wearing a spotted apron and a spuriously jovial air. "Top o' the day to ye, Mr. Pritchett. Yer usual, sir?"

Pritchett took his pint to one of the small tables. In a far corner of the room, several natty lads and lasses were engaged in a noisy gambling game. Children of the rookeries these were, who learned to beg and steal when they could barely crawl.

A girl disengaged herself from the group, a mere slip of a thing with an untidy mop of hair that was dark blonde or light brown depending on how recently she had washed it — she hadn't washed it all that recently, Pritchett noted — and dark eyes set in a face so nondescript that she could pass as a parson's daughter or a bit o' muslin, a pot boy or a flower girl. In the unlikely case she was caught out, she carried a wicked blade tucked away under her clothes.

Pritchett didn't know her age. Frankie might be as old as sixteen. Today she looked like a shop girl.

He slid the pint toward her. She drank thirstily. "Ta, guv."

Conversation buzzed around them. Even in surroundings such as these, the business of the Queen was on every lip. Those who could, read the newssheets aloud to those who couldn't, on street corners and in coffee houses, taverns and subscription rooms.

Frankie wiped her sleeve across her mouth. Pritchett said, "I have a job of work for you."

She held out her hand. "Don't be close-fisted, guv."

This enterprising little tatterdemalion, reflected Pritchett, was almost as venal as he was himself.

He dropped a guinea on her palm. She bit the coin then, satisfied, tucked it into her bodice and leaned closer. "Let's have it," she said.

'Let's have it', indeed. At a nearby table — not too close yet not too far away — a fair-haired man slouched in a chair, a glass on the table before him, his hat pulled low on his brow; a most unremarkable, undistinguishable sort of fellow come out to wet his whistle with rotgut gin.

Appearances were deceiving. The Deacon never drank. The Deacon watched, and listened, and plotted out his wicked schemes.

Chapter Five

It is foolish to tear one's hair in grief, as though sorrow would be made less by baldness. — Cicero

Clea's carriage drew up in front of a stately house in fashionable Harley Street, a red brick structure embellished with hipped roof and sash windows and neat white pillars. Her footman leapt down to lower the steps and open the carriage door. "I believe I prefer Wakely Court," commented Senhora Estevez. "It does not gaze so sternly down upon one. Are you certain this is a good idea?"

"I subscribe to the Strategic Offensive Principle of War. Otherwise known as doing unto others before they can do unto you." Clea stepped down into the street. She was keenly aware of her surroundings, and the weight of the small Spanish pistol currently residing in her reticule.

Harry had presented her with that little pistol.

Ironic that she felt she might have need of it in his mama's house.

The footman mounted the steps leading to the Marsden residence, briskly assaulted the brass knocker. The front door opened to reveal a white-haired manservant whose posture was as rigid as if he had whalebone built into his livery. He looked at the women, blinked, then looked at them again, mouth slightly agape.

Clea could hardly blame him. Pilar was a sight not soon forgot. Today Senhora Estevez had chosen a cone-shaped dress fashioned of brightly colored stripes that ran in different directions on the skirt, hem and sleeves; a deep red shawl with a paisley patterned border; and a broad-brimmed bonnet trimmed in plaid ribbon that tied under her chin.

Pilar liked bright patterns. It mattered not a whit to her whether or not those patterns matched.

Clea took pity on the butler. "Good afternoon, Williams. I trust Mrs. Williams is well? Pray remember me to her."

The butler tore his fascinated gaze away from the senhora. "She is in excellent health, thank you, Lady Clea. And if I may say so as shouldn't, she'll be pleased you asked. The mistress is expecting you. If you will follow me—" He escorted the women into the first floor drawing room and left them there to cool their heels.

Glass chandeliers hung from the elaborate plaster ceiling. A correspondingly ornate carpet lay on the polished wooden floor. The room was furnished with an abundance of pier tables, a commode and an elegant fire screen; a gilt suite consisting of large and small sofas, a confidante and armchair. All incorporated scrolled endpieces and straight legs and were adorned with flutings, paterae, palm leaves, and honeysuckle. Above the massive overmantel hung a mirror which reflected a host of small ornaments and a great ormolu clock. "*Santo Deus*," Pilar breathed.

A thin, mauve-clad woman entered the room. Her silver hair was arranged in soft waves and twisted up at her nape. Lines of discontent marred what might once have been a lovely face.

Her grey eyes fixed on Clea, eyes so familiar that Clea experienced a pang of regret.

Where Harry's eyes had been filled with warmth and laughter, however, his mother's were cold as frost. "It is good of you to see us," Clea said, when her mama-in-law failed to speak. "Pray permit me to present Senhora Pilar Estevez, who has come with me from Portugal. Pilar, this is Harry's mama, Mrs. Marsden, of whom you heard him often speak."

"I am pleased to make your acquaintance, Mrs. Marsden." Pilar dropped a pretty curtsey, exquisitely polite.

The older woman's nostrils flared, as if her sensibilities were offended by a female who had such original notions about appropriate attire. "A pity I cannot say the same. Send this person away, Clea. What I have to say to you is for your ears alone."

Since her mama-in-law clearly preferred she didn't, Clea sat down on the confidante. "I have no secrets from Pilar."

"Be it on your head." Mrs. Marsden lowered herself stiffly to the edge of an opposing chair. "I shall never understand why Harold married you. He could have had the daughter of a duke."

Pilar remained standing, by one of the tall windows. "*Un minuto, por favor*. Is not the sister of an earl almost as desirable as the daughter of a duke?"

Mrs. Marsden's nostrils flared. "It depends on the earl. An exploring officer who spent the war skulking about behind enemy lines while braver men marched out to face their deaths— One is hardly eager to welcome a spy into one's family."

Clea clamped her teeth together. Mrs. Marsden's youngest son had enjoyed his share of clandestine adventures at Wellington's behest. But because Harry would not have wished it, Clea did not inform his mama that her youngest son had frequently and cheerfully set about doing things she would have disliked.

Harry had been destined for a brilliant military career from the moment of his birth, his position secured through strings pulled and favors owed.

"Do pay attention, Clea!" Mariel rapped her knuckles against the arm of her chair. "I cannot conceive why Harold decided to revisit that horrid place. But he went, against my advice, and look what came of it."

"Portugal is a lovely country!" objected Pilar. "As for your son's desire to return, few men survive a war unchanged. The excitement, the adventure, the constant awareness of danger and death. For some, it was the first time they truly felt alive."

"Utter nonsense!" declared Mrs. Marsden. "Harold was not such a—"

"Cod's head?" supplied Clea. Her mama-in-law flinched. "Harry wanted to go travelling, and so we did." As had countless other tourists, Europe having been off limits during twenty long years of war.

Unlike those other tourists, Harry had not returned.

Clea had buried him in the little cemetery at Frenada and remained there with him until she had no choice but to depart.

"Nor do I understand why you didn't have the decency to bring my son home." Mariel continued, "You should have done so at once."

Clea offered no defense. Coming back to London had required that she pick up the threads of her old life.

The senhora cleared her throat. "In my country we have a saying: Delayed is preferable to never. Clea is here now."

"So I see," said Mrs. Marsden. "And I wish that I did not."

"I am observing the proprieties," Clea informed her. "As I am told I should. What did you say to Hannah to put her in such a tweak?"

Mariel sat up even straighter in her chair. "Harold claimed that you are clever. I do not agree. A clever person would be aware that someone as familiar with firearms as my son is unlikely to have accidentally shot himself. But if Harry *was* so careless, I've no doubt it may be laid at your doorstep. I cannot credit that you were a sympathetic spouse."

Clea, were she not determined to behave in a relatively unaggressive manner, might have pointed out that Mrs. Marsden's own unlamented husband had, according to the gossips, hardly behaved in the manner of a gentleman with a 'sympathetic spouse'. "If you are suggesting your son was unhappy in his marriage, I assure you he was not."

Mariel regarded her with distaste. "A lady does not speak of such matters. But then, you are hardly a lady. They say you shot a highwayman on your way into town."

"Merely in the shoulder!" Pilar interjected. "Me, I think she should have shot the *malfeitor* dead."

Mrs. Marsden disregarded this unsolicited opinion. "Harry possessed a pair of dueling pistols that were given him by his father. I would like to have them back."

"Harry's dueling pistols?" Clea repeated, startled by this change of subject. "Surely they must be the last thing you want."

The older woman's hands tightened on the arms of her chair. "Those pistols are of great sentimental value. You cannot be so selfish as to keep all Harold's possessions for yourself."

Selfish? Maybe Clea was. She was also wary of this display of maternal emotion from a woman who had none. "Harry resided in this house until we wed. Surely you can find some other item of 'great sentimental value' among the things he left behind."

Mariel's gaze sharpened. "Before you set out on your wedding trip,

Harold arranged for his personal belongings to be boxed up and sent to your brother's house. Odd that he neglected to tell you that. Since it is obvious you care nothing for my feelings—" She rose and tugged the bellpull. "Williams will see you out."

Chapter Six

A coward turns away, but a brave man's choice is danger.
— Euripides

Baron Saxe strolled down St James's Street toward White's, London's oldest and most prestigious gentleman's club. Behind that handsome and well-proportioned narrow brick façade, those Corinthian pilasters, wealthy lords wagered deeply night and day.

He exchanged a few words with the doorman, nodded to the hall porter, handed his hat to a turbaned Negro page.

White's provided its members with surroundings as luxurious as their own homes: thick carpets and marble fireplaces, fine crystal, richly upholstered furniture. Kane skirted the bow window where a few years past Brummel had lounged, in company with Alvanley and Sefton and occasionally the Duke of Argyle, amusing himself by placing wagers on one thing and another and making unkind remarks about the shoppers who passed by outside. The table in front of the bow window was these days reserved for the Duke of Wellington, who was not currently seated there.

Few of the club members were in attendance at the moment. Gentlemen who played till dawn could hardly be expected to rise before mid-afternoon. Kane chose a secluded corner and a comfortable arm-chair. A waiter appeared promptly with a tray bearing a bottle and a glass.

Not long ago, Kane would not have imbibed of the grape so early. These days, he was tempted to call for a bottle the moment he left his bed. He lifted his glass and drank, thinking of his inamorata, whom he had not seen for several days.

He doubted she had missed him. Lilah had hired a chemist and was busily concocting nostrums to preserve complexions, remove wrinkles, restore — by means of gall nuts and willow charcoal, lead ore, ebony chips, nitrate of silver and sulfate of copper — the color of one's hair, all of which seemed remarkably optimistic at a time when half the population feared an uprising and the other half looked forward to the same. Still, Kane and Mrs. Kingston had a relationship of long standing, and even if he did not especially enjoy being told that urine mixed with rose water was an excellent aid to feminine beauty, for example, she ranked high among his friends and he must make up for his neglect.

What did one give the abbess who had everything? Another jewel, another expensive bauble? Lilah would thank him politely and toss his offering into a drawer.

She would like a virgin better.

Kane couldn't imagine where he would locate one of those.

That reflection led him to Clea, who surely was a virgin no longer, and he really, really mustn't dwell on *that*.

Once, a younger Clea had aspired to a career as an acknowledged beauty, with dozens of gentlemen dangling at her slipper-strings, writing her poems, and doing the various foolish things that love-sick young pups were prone to do. Kane wondered how many hearts she might break now that she had come back to town, and if breaking hearts was what she wanted, although what she wanted would matter little to the men who'd flocked around her at the theater, and who were doubtless showering her with flowers, pretty presents, billets-doux.

Kane had never been so young, or moon-mad, as to pen a billet-doux.

Nor had he ever received a love letter, unless one counted impassioned invitations to assignations, which he did not.

Odd, now, to question what else he might have missed.

So unsettling were these ruminations that the baron was almost relieved when a fair-haired, grey-eyed, middle-aged man appropriated the nearest chair.

Amory Marsden was not a man attuned to his fellows, in this instance a fellow who demonstrated little desire to engage in conversation. "I had hoped to find you here, Saxe. Have you seen the latest entries in the betting book? There can remain little question but that the Milan Commission went too far in their efforts to oblige."

At White's, members could wager on anything that took their fancy. Entries in the club's betting book included births and deaths and marriages; the outcome of the latest scandal; the length of a friend's life or of a ministry; and, most recently, the business of a Queen.

Kane felt a headache forming behind his right eye.

Princess Caroline's unconventional conduct had agitated Lord Liverpool and other members of the government for some time. The Milan Commission had been set up, at the Prince Regent's insistence, to sniff out evidence of her adultery. As result of the commissioners' enthusiastic efforts, a host of Italian workmen, painters and boatmen had come forward to spin tales of the Queen and Pergami conducting themselves like lovers during the day as well as making elaborate preparations to avoid being interrupted at night.

Amory was still talking. "For the Bill to pass, the allegations against the Queen must be proved to the satisfaction of both Houses of Parliament. You must surely realize that even if the Bill does pass the Lords, it is highly unlikely to pass the Commons as well."

Silently, Kane sipped his drink. He realized many things, among them that Amory Marsden hadn't interrupted his solitude to discuss the Queen.

The man bore little resemblance to his younger brother. Where Harry Marsden had been dashing and adventurous, handsome, quick to laugh — and an amiable companion, one assumed, else Clea wouldn't have married him — Amory was serious and reserved, with prematurely lined features and stooped shoulders that gave the impression he carried around the weight of the world.

To some extent, he did. Amory Marsden was so prominent a member of the Lower House that more than one attempt had been made on his life. Kane said, "Caroline and Pergami *and* the Milan Commission may take themselves to Hades. Now that we have dispensed with the preliminaries, what is it you came to speak with me about?"

Amory glanced around, lowered his voice. "I had intended to be more subtle, but have it as you wish. This concerns the Fairchild family."

Kane contemplated his empty glass. "Why am I not surprised?"

Amory beckoned the waiter to fetch another bottle. "My mother is, as the colonials might put it, on the warpath. On the one hand, she is angry that Lady Clea has had the gall to return to London, thereby reminding Maman of her loss. On the other, she is equally furious that my brother's widow didn't bring him home with her."

Kane was visited by a horrific vision of Clea traveling with a decomposing corpse. "I see."

Amory said, wearily, "I rather doubt you do. My mother is dissatisfied with the accounts of my brother's death. She is determined to have his body exhumed. I have told her numerous times that I refuse to arrange anything of the sort. Unfortunately, the fact that I have managed to circumvent her for the moment doesn't that mean Maman won't try to have someone else tend to the business. I'm hoping you might use your influence to prevent such an event taking place."

Kane frequently marveled at the miracles people expected him to accomplish. "You don't want your brother returned?"

"I want my brother back. That being impossible, I would prefer his bones be left undisturbed." The waiter rejoined them. Amory paused while he poured. "It's not like Maman doted on Harry. Beyond what we may do for her, she doesn't like any of us much."

There were two Marsden sisters, Kane recalled, neither of whom resided in London. The gossips claimed they had deliberately contracted marriages that would remove them from under their mother's tyrannical thumb.

"Harry can no longer advance the family's fortunes," Amory continued. "Maman holds his widow to blame. I'd like to say my mother is unhinged by grief, but she has always been unreasonable. It would make all our lives easier if you persuaded Lady Clea to adopt a more conciliatory attitude."

Conciliatory? Clea?

Life was growing complicated. Kane wished that *he* might travel. To the Americas. China. Maybe the North Pole.

Chapter Seven

Come back. Even as a shadow, even as a dream. —
Euripides

Clea threaded a pathway way through the abandoned miscellanea that cluttered the attics of Wakely Court. Light shone dimly through small windows set high in the walls.

She passed by an embossed leather box, its wooden legs connected by iron crossbars, that she hadn't seen before; skirted a battered suit of armor — where had Ned, or more likely Julie, discovered *that*? — and made her way toward the crates and boxes stacked in a cleared space near the far wall.

Tidcombe had known exactly where Harry's things were stored. When Clea asked why he hadn't informed her of their presence, he'd responded that it was hardly his place.

The butler had grown no fonder of her, Clea concluded, while she'd been away.

Ordinarily, attics were stifling hot. These attics were cold as the tomb. Or they were today, at any rate. Clea peered into the shadows, regretting that she had not brought a lantern with her. One could all too easily imagine sinister shapes stirring amid the forest of forgotten things.

If any old pile was truly haunted, it would be Wakely Court.

In memory she saw a silhouetted figure on horseback atop a distant hillock, spyglass in hand.

A whisper of noise, a flicker of movement— Clea took firmer hold of her little Spanish pistol. "Harry?" she said out loud.

Claws scrabbled against the old wooden floorboards, followed by a thud, a quickly silenced squeak.

Pilar had remained below, vowing she would be fatigued beyond bearing if forced to climb so many stairs. Nor had she been eager to acquaint herself, she'd added, with several centuries' accumulation of cobwebs and dust. But the senhora was not wholly without fellow feeling. She'd sent Fausto along for company.

Clea put down her pistol and dragged the largest trunk into a patch of daylight. Dust motes rose and settled. She sneezed.

Why had Harry had his belongings sent to Ned's house?

Probably because he preferred that his possessions be kept from his mother's prying eyes.

Clea knelt on the floor in front of the trunk, threw open the lid.

Scarlet fabric. Brass buttons. Fringed epaulettes and gold braid. She unfolded Harry's uniform jacket and pressed it to her face ...

All Europe was gathered in Vienna. Every sovereign whose fortunes had been affected by the Napoleonic Wars, with their courts and sycophants; people who had business at the Congress and even more who did not; political groups who sought recognition from the great lords. Vienna's promenades and squares were thick with soldiers wearing the uniforms of the European armies and swarms of aristocratic servants in their splendid liveries, as well as a mob of uninvolved observers who had been drawn there by the drama, a hundred thousand strong. People crowded to catch a momentary glimpse of some military sovereign or diplomatic celebrity— Czar Alexander of Russia, Talleyrand, Metternich. Prince Esterhazy, wearing pearl pendants on his boots and an aigrette of gems in his headgear.

After nightfall the theaters, cafes and public resorts had teemed with pleasure-seeking crowds. Magnificent carriages traversed the city in every direction, on their way to grand routs at the Imperial Palace, concerts and balls. In almost every thoroughfare, musicians played. Even though she turned sixteen during those five months, Ned had considered Clea too young to attend many of the festivities. He'd expected her to be content with observing a military festival in celebration of the peace; hearing Handel's great oratorio *Samson* sung by a chorus of five hundred voices at the Burg; attending a popular festival in the Augarten, during which the crowd grew so unruly that many prominent women went home with their clothing torn and minus many of their gems.

She hadn't been content. And Harry hadn't considered her too young. He'd introduced Clea to the excitement of a masked ball. Somewhere amidst the polonaise and minuet and waltz, she'd tumbled headfirst into love.

Ned had felt she was too young for that also. Consequently, Clea hadn't wed until she was eighteen.

The next year, she'd been widowed. Two years later, she was kneeling in the dust of Wakely Court's cluttered attics, staining Harry's scarlet jacket with her tears.

This accomplishes nothing, she scolded herself. Clea folded the jacket and set it aside before digging deeper into the trunk, uncertain of what she sought. There would be little to comfort a grieving mother among these relics of the Peninsular War.

Her fingers closed around a small battered notebook, the sort that might fit in a man's pocket. Clea flipped through the pages, found a combination of notes and diagrams and numbers written in an unfamiliar hand.

She heard footsteps, coming closer. Clea closed the notebook and shoved it back into the trunk; snatched up her little gun and scrambled to her feet.

Kane emerged from the shadows. He paused, eyes fixed on the pistol. "Am I to be next?"

Clea lowered her weapon. "You may commend me for my restraint. Despite immense provocation, I haven't shot anyone for several days."

A clatter, a crash. In a blur of blue-grey fur, Fausto leapt up on a dusty oak sideboard. Kane demanded, "What the deuce is *that*?"

"His name is Fausto, which means fortunate." Clea winced as a tureen crashed to the floor. "Fortunate for whom, I cannot say."

Fausto disappeared behind an ancient oak wardrobe.

Kane bent and picked up pieces of pottery from the floor. "I didn't realize that you are fond of cats."

Clea closed the trunk. "I'm not. Shouldn't you be out about government business? I suppose Tidcombe told you where I was."

"Occasionally I manage a few moments for business of my own." Kane set the shards aside, pulled a handkerchief from the pocket of his coat. "I haven't yet told you that I'm sorry for your loss."

'Business', was she? Clea took his handkerchief. Kane would be accustomed to damp-faced females. The man must have inspired veritable floods of tears during his long rakehelly career.

He picked up a footstool embroidered with roses, daisies and strawberry blossoms, shook off the dust, and placed it on the floor in front of her. "Sit," he said.

Clea lowered herself onto the stool. Kane reached out and cupped her cheek.

Startled, Clea stared up at him. He plucked a cobweb from her hair.

Before she could react, Kane stepped back. "We need to talk."

So they did, conceded Clea. And so she would, once she got over being dumbstruck by the sensation of Kane's fingers against her face.

With the simple touch of his hand, he had recalled the girl she had once been, when her romantic daydreams had revolved around him.

He leaned against the trunk. "Tell me about your husband. I didn't know him well."

Clea wrenched her gaze away from Kane, stared instead at a moth-eaten tapestry of huntsmen shooting water fowl. Or maybe the men were shooting rabbits. Due to the ravages of time, the nature of their quarry was difficult to ascertain.

"Trust me," Kane said.

Trust this hardened breaker of female hearts? Oddly, Clea did.

"Harry was two people," she said slowly. "I'm not sure *I* knew either of them well. On the one hand, he was cheerful and charming. On the other, he was prone to black moods and depression and night terrors, when he recognized no one and friends turned into enemies."

"Even you?" asked Kane.

"No, never. Or almost never." Some memories were better not revisited. Clea applied Kane's handkerchief briskly to her nose.

"I know this isn't easy," he told her. "It's important or I wouldn't ask."

Easy? Rather, it was like peeling back her skin to leave every nerve exposed. "Harry's temper grew increasingly uncertain as we traveled through the Peninsula. In Lisbon, he encountered an acquaintance embarked on a similar tour of battlefields. They spent several pleasant hours exchanging reminiscences. Or so he told me, and I believed him at the time."

Had there been some indication of what was to come? Something that she'd missed?

Kane urged, "Go on."

Lord Saxe, the interrogator, thought Clea. He'd give her no peace until she did as he wished.

Not that 'peace' was an emotion commonly associated with Kane.

"Lately I've begun to suspect those reminiscences weren't all that pleasant," she admitted. "Harry had something weighing on his mind. That last night he went out for a purpose, but I have no idea what it was."

"Boatmen found him the next morning by the Tagus River, dead from a pistol shot to the head," Kane supplied, when she again fell silent. "His death was deemed an accident, though there were rumors of suicide."

Clea crumpled the handkerchief in her hands. "You are well-informed."

"Would you expect anything less?" Kane scooped up another piece of broken pottery. "Amory Marsden approached me at White's."

That explained why he was here. Clea blew out an exasperated breath. "Mariel has always held me in aversion. There's no need for you to involve yourself in this affair."

Kane didn't immediately answer. Clea regretted that she hadn't chosen a different word. 'Business,' she should have said. 'Headache.' 'Hornet's nest.' Anything that did not remind them both of his fingers touching her face.

He set the shard beside the others on a dusty crate. "Amory requested that I convey a warning. He recommends that you be more conciliatory. It seems that his mother has taken a maggot into her head."

"Pardon!" Pilar emerged from behind the coat of arms, causing them both to start. "You are speaking of Mistress Marsden? A *louva-a-*

deus, that one, an insect that eats its young. Or do I mean its mate? Tidcombe told me you had a caller, *querida.* A respectable young widow should not be closeted with a gentleman unchaperoned." She awarded Kane a flirtatious glance. "One does not aspire to be thought of as a chaperone, *naturalmente,* but a lady's good name must be safeguarded. Or so the dowager Dorset has explained. Me, I was the mistress of a *bandido.* I do not understand these things."

"Permit me to introduce you," Clea said wryly, and did so. Pilar was in remarkably good spirits despite the dust and dirt swirling around her, and after having climbed all those fatiguing stairs. The senhora fluttered her eyelashes. The baron murmured all that was polite.

Fausto emerged from the shadows, a limp-tailed corpse dangling from his jaws. He dropped the mouse at his mistress's feet. Pilar bent and picked up the cat, in the process affording an illuminating glimpse of her bosom, magnificently displayed by décolletage that earlier had not plunged quite so low.

Moreover, Clea noted, she had discarded her matronly lace cap.

Unaccountably annoyed by the appreciative gleam in Kane's eye, Clea thrust his handkerchief back into his hand. "What is this warning Amory wanted you to convey?"

He did not look so amused now. "Mariel Marsden is threatening to open a formal inquiry into her son's death."

Chapter Eight

Let each man pass his days in that wherein his skill is
greatest. — Sextus

Frankie bit into an apple as she strolled along narrow Rosemary Lane. The street's sweet-smelling name was made a mockery by less-than-fragrant fumes rising from filthy rags and ancient shoes. London's poor met at the Rag Fair to sell tattered garments that were marginally finer than those they wore on their backs, and also to buy and sell stolen goods.

The narrow lane was crammed with people. Broad-boughed bawds and bone-idle beggars smoked and shouted, bargained, guzzled coffee and tea and sometimes beer. Frankie brushed past dollymops and magsmen and half-naked brats; dubbers and duffers and angling coves; raggedy ex-soldiers and sharp-eyed operators who could steal and sell the coat off a person's back in less than a trice.

Secondhand shops lined both sides of the street. Tables and baskets were set up on the edge of the pavement, in front of windows and doors. Goods were hung in stalls or piled on barrows; draped over old chairs and clothes-horses; spread out on the ground, on pieces of matting or carpet or straw. Frankie paid sharp heed to her feet lest she trample some of the wares. She was just another wagtail in patched skirts and threadbare shawl today, face unrecognizable under a thick coating of grease and grime, hair stuffed up under a filthy straw hat.

A razor-sharp folding knife tucked up her sleeve where no one could see.

She'd had the weapon off a soldier recently returned from Spain. A *navaja*, he'd said it was. Frankie had bought it from him proper. A girl needed to protect herself whilst about Mr. Pritchett's little chores.

Frankie did all sort of chores for Mr. Pritchett. Currently, he had her keeping a watchful eye out, to which end she needed to spruce up her wardrobe.

What Mr. Pritchett did with the information she provided him, Frankie didn't know and didn't care.

The Runner was busy these days, he claimed, tracking down the source of the queer banknotes that were making the bigwigs at the Bank of England cross as a cageful of wet cats.

Pritchett was doing nothing of the sort. Frankie had figured that much out.

Having finished off her apple — which mere moments past had rested alongside others in a coster's cart, Frankie making a habit of keeping her skills sharp — she tossed the core aside, paused to rummage through a pile of boots. A clever cobbler could join several broken shoes together to make a serviceable whole. Finding nothing she cared to purchase, she next inspected an old silk hat with the nap stripped off, its glossy black turned into a whitish brown. A handkerchief picked from someone's pocket. A parson's bonnet, probably snatched right off his head. Frankie herself was mighty slick at bonnet-snatching. Today, however, she kept her daddles to herself.

Frankie knew a great deal about pickpockets, knuckles, dippers, having caught the eye of a kidsman called Old Ikey when she was knee-high to a duck. Ikey trained up young operators, trading food and shelter for whatever pilfered items they brought home. Those who came back empty-handed were turned out into the cold until they stole enough to pay their shot.

Old Ikey had been — still was, for all Frankie knew — about as soft-hearted as a stone.

A cribbage-faced Captain Queernabs flashed his ivories at her. Frankie tossed her head and flounced on down the lane. She purchased a pair of worsted stockings for a penny, a black cloth waistcoat for three and a petticoat for seven, then paused to refresh herself with a pint of beer purchased from one of the alehouses that lined the lane.

The seller threw her coin on the counter, testing to see if it would break in half, the fashioning of sixpence pieces requiring only a chalk mold, a pewter tankard, and a small crucible.

Clipping, filing metal from the edges of coins, was the most common form of coining. So long as enough of the face of a coin was left that it would be recognized, it generally passed muster.

As in this case.

Frankie paid one shilling for a pint of ale and received ten pence halfpenny in change.

From the shadows of a stall where hundreds of battered bonnets hung suspended by strings, a fair-haired man watched Frankie drink her pint, wipe her mouth on her sleeve.

Business had brought the Deacon to Whitechapel. He'd been not far from the Royal Mint when he'd spied the girl sauntering by. She had a certain way of walking that betrayed her, whatever rags she wore, and he had a keen eye.

He also had a notion Frankie might be put to his own good use, once Pritchett was persuaded to part with her.

The Runner was too valuable a tool to alienate just yet.

The Deacon hadn't risen to his current position by ignoring his instincts, which were currently telling him Frankie didn't want to be recognized. And so he'd followed her to the Rag Fair, which had necessitated purchasing a cloak fit only for a scarecrow to throw around his shoulders, and trading his fine beaver hat for a filthy felt cap, and stepping deliberately in noxious puddles to muddy his boots as he trailed her through dunghills of tatters and shreds.

Frankie bought a pair of white cotton braces for a penny, exchanged another coin, continued on down the lane.

The Deacon stepped out of his hiding place, setting the bonnets swaying as if from a violent breeze.

He wondered if Pritchett knew that his *protégée* was busily exchanging false coins for true. Or if he'd put her up to it himself.

Easier for a camel to pass through the eye of a needle than for a rich man to enter the kingdom of heaven. The Deacon hadn't the least interest into getting into heaven. He had a great deal of interest, however, in becoming very, very rich.

Chapter Nine

As you sow, so shall you reap. — Cicero

Baron Saxe had set out for Gentleman Jackson's Boxing Saloon in Bond Street with every intention of improving his frame of mind — the baron remained in tiptop physical condition as result of regular pugilistic exercise that had the additional benefit of relieving the frustrations attendant upon his involvement in affairs of state. Fortunately for the continued well-being of today's prospective sparring partners, Kane encountered an acquaintance and was soon thereafter accompanying him into one of the numerous establishments where coffee and chocolate and other refreshments were served.

The front window of the large room was filled with cups and pots and strainers of a dozen different designs. The wooden floor was worn with use, the ceiling low-beamed. Off that floor, and walls, and ceiling, bounced countless conversations, the patrons of the coffee house vigorously voicing their opinions of what they had read in the latest newssheets, along with extensive speculation regarding, primarily, the fate of the Queen.

Kane was heartily tired of hearing about the Queen, whom he blamed for his current ill temper.

Partly, at any rate.

Neither Prinny nor his Princess could be fairly held responsible for the fact that Kane found himself thinking too often of Clea Fairchild, even though he knew damned well he should not.

He'd found her kneeling before an open trunk in Wakely Court's dusty attics. At sight of her weeping, Kane had wished to gnash his teeth.

No, if he were honest — and if he could not be honest with himself, then who — Kane had wished to set Clea on his lap and distract her by means of a brisk tumble, but had possessed sufficient presence of mind to present her with his handkerchief instead.

He recalled the smoothness of her cheek under his hand. Would her skin elsewhere be as silky and soft? Or even more so?

Mentally, Kane kicked himself.

Apparently, while he wasn't paying attention, he had degenerated into a randy old *roué*.

Silently, he led the way to a small round table placed near the back wall. A waiter arrived, carrying steaming coffee in two shallow delftware bowls. Kane requested a brandy and water instead.

His companion reached for a cup of coffee. "Granted, the spirit of the time is most alarming but are matters so bad as that?"

Matters were indeed, alas. "Liverpool and the ministers visited the King at Windsor in an effort to persuade him to abandon the Bill's divorce clause. Prinny listened, said 'Do as you please' and sent them on their way without even an offer of refreshment. Meantime, Wellington is concerned that among the large crowds gathering in favor of the Queen are countless dissatisfied ex-soldiers trained in the use of arms. On a lighter note, Sidmouth recently received an anonymous missive warning him to be on the alert because a thousand prostitutes of the lowest order have taken up Caroline's cause."

Kane paused as the waiter returned with his brandy and water. His companion looked mildly amused. Giles Lawrence was a man of medium height and stature, approximately Kane's age. Close-cropped prematurely grey hair accented the harsh lines of his face, his sharp cheekbones and lean jaw.

Kane took a swallow of his drink. In almost the same moment, Giles pushed his coffee cup aside. "You are ignoring me. I dislike to be ignored. It does a man of your position no credit to succumb to the sullens, Saxe."

"I am not in the sullens," Kane growled.

"I misspoke," Giles said smoothly. "You are merely sulky as a bear. Granted, the abominably poor taste currently being displayed by the

Royal Family is enough to put anyone off his feed. One expects better of the monarchy than to be boring on about their squalid little intrigues. I have nothing against intrigues, squalid or otherwise, you understand; it is the airing of dirty linen to which I take offense. Do not bother to tell me to confine myself to my own business. My mind is of an inquisitive structure, as you will have heard."

"I have heard many things," Kane responded. "I do you the courtesy of dismissing the majority of them out of hand."

"The majority of them," Giles repeated. "I find myself mildly curious about what you chose to believe."

"The worst, of course."

Giles smiled. "*Touché.* Tell me, how does the lovely Mrs. Kingston these days?"

Instructions for enlarging the male member: rub your penis with wasp stings and massage it with sweet oil. When it swells, let it dangle for ten nights through a hole in your bed.

Kane grimaced. "Lilah has expanded her sphere of operations. She is now providing cosmetics to half the town."

"From the *Kama Sutra* to *The Toilet of Flora*," Giles marveled. "One has to admire her resourcefulness."

Mr. Lawrence was fairly resourceful himself. As result of his unending efforts to avoid boredom, he had come to function as a sort of inquiry agent to the *ton.* Giles dealt with blackmailers and elopements; retrieved misplaced spouses, heiresses, and valuables as well. Recently, he had recovered a painting — Rembrandt's *Self Portrait in a Flat Cap,* oil on canvas — that had been brazenly removed from Carleton House.

Kane imagined Giles's response to a red-faced Prinny stomping his foot and shrieking 'I want my Rembrandt back!'

Giles sighed. "You are determined to be disobliging. I suppose I should not scold you for it, being as the Queen's trial will shortly resume."

Kane disliked to contemplate the trial's resumption, and the attendant uproar. Frequently of late he longed for a world where black was black and white was white and there were no shades of gray. Where kings and queens didn't act like spoiled children, and warring political factions didn't seize upon any opportunity to point fingers and call names.

Where dashing young lieutenants didn't shoot themselves and accidents were exactly what they seemed.

"Not that I care one way or another," Giles added. "In my opinion, our less-than-beloved King deserves to be saddled with his unappealing Queen. Let us speak of more important matters. I saw you in conversation with Amory Marsden at White's. You appeared out of sorts."

"I daresay that I did."

"I disremember when I have had such difficulty holding someone's interest," Giles lamented. "Must I stand on my head?"

"I beg you will not."

Mr. Lawrence steepled his elegant fingers together. "Permit me to advance our conversation. You did not bring me here for the quality of the refreshment, I conjecture, but so we might speak without being overheard."

So Kane had, but he was belatedly questioning the impulse.

The devil with it, he decided. In for a penny, in for a pound. "How well are you acquainted with the Marsden family?"

" 'Look like the innocent flower, but be the serpent under it,' " Giles recited. "Were Shakespeare among us, he would put the matriarch in a play. Mariel Marsden took to her bed for a week after young Harry defied the desires of his family and made a love match."

Kane almost sympathized. He too had taken to bed after being told of Clea's marriage, for reasons he did not care to closely consider, but the bed hadn't been his own.

"She has not altered her opinion. Mrs. Marsden nourishes a strong antipathy toward her younger son's widow," he said.

"I do hope you are more direct than this in your diplomatic dealings," Giles remarked. "What is it you want of me?"

"I'm not entirely certain." Kane repeated Clea's comments about her husband's final days. "Mariel might not be far off the mark when she claims there is something strange about her son's death."

"Then again, she may be," commented Giles. "The woman is deranged. If you like, I will pursue the matter on Lady Clea's behalf."

Kane had been involved in political maneuverings fall too long to trust this easy acquiescence. "Why so agreeable?" he asked.

Giles shrugged. "Why not?"

"You are not telling me everything, I think."

"My good man," said Giles gently. "Whyever would you expect I should?

Chapter Ten

Luck is what happens when preparation meets
opportunity. — Seneca

When accused of misbehavior of one manner or another, Senhora Estevez announced with the assurance of one who knew whereof she spoke, a lady should immediately enact insouciance for the benefit of as large an audience as could be contrived. Her friend's objections to a public demonstration, she languidly waved aside. If anyone tried to interfere with them, she said, it would provide Clea a perfect opportunity to shoot off her little gun.

Once inspired to action, the senhora exerted herself amazingly. Consequently, Lady Clea found herself examining the attractions at a Ladies' Bazaar for the Sale of Miscellaneous Articles, a sort of indoors street with shops and stalls where attendants vied to draw her attention to their wares while nimble-fingered shoplifters made off with toys and trinkets and more than one careless patron's purse.

At length, after some last-minute parlaying with a purveyor of ribbon and silk netting, Pilar pronounced herself fatigued. Trailed by the footman who had accompanied them on this outing, his person currently draped about with packages like a Christmas tree, the ladies returned to their vehicle and set out in search of a rejuvenating ice.

Clea stared out the carriage window. She might have enjoyed the outing, save for the now familiar itch between her shoulder blades that warned of hostile eyes.

But whose?

She glanced around, saw nothing untoward.

The cobbled streets were thronged with traffic, both vehicular and pedestrian, the citizenry encouraged to venture forth by faint indications that the sun might finally emerge from behind the clouds. Vendors worked their way through the crowd, hawking everything from hot chestnuts to lavender for use in the linen press. Running patterers peddled one-penny broadsides and penny-a-yard ballads, the current favorite being 'The British Seamen and their Beloved Queen'; shouted out the latest Banbury tale that was being passing off as news. Those same zealous news-sellers had several years before proclaimed Napoleon Bonaparte's escape from St. Helena in a balloon, and declared that a local butcher was filling his sausages with human flesh.

Hannah would have palpitations, thought Clea, were a Dorset to be pilloried in the press.

Adopt a more conciliatory attitude, Amory Marsden had suggested. Clea would adopt a more conciliatory attitude when pigs learned to fly.

The carriage swung into Berkeley Square, a wide street flanked by long ranges of stone-fronted terrace houses laid out early in the previous century. An oval garden with long borders, in its center a pump house with a Chinese roof, ran parallel to the structures on each side.

The square swarmed with gentlefolk who had come out to enjoy the confections provided by Gunter's Tea Shop, centered on the square's east side. Ladies in fashionable muslin dresses, their elegant equipages drawn up in the shade of the plane maple trees, posed prettily for gentlemen who lounged against iron park railings and paid them pretty compliments. Waiters scurried back and forth across the busy street, risking life and limb to deliver delicacies that started to melt the instant they were taken from their molds.

Pilar professed herself possessed of a huge hunger. Being, she asserted, of an inquiring nature, she was determined to inspect the icehouse in the shop's cellars where the confections were made. Clea must accompany her, moreover; one did not convey insouciance by cowering inside a carriage, after all.

Clea looped her reticule over her wrist, stepped down from the carriage and out into the street. Pilar followed, attracting no little attention to herself. Today the senhora's splendid figure was displayed to excellent advantage in a walking dress made up in bright yellow muslin. On her dark curls rested a large-brimmed straw bonnet, trimmed with silk flowers, feathers, and lace. To protect her complexion from the detrimental effects of sunlight, not that the sun had yet deigned to put in an appearance, she carried a pretty parasol.

She fluttered her eyelashes at the footman, who blushed, and lazily engaged him in a conversation suited neither to her position nor his.

Pilar, as Clea well knew, could not help but flirt.

She recalled, with renewed annoyance, how Pilar had flirted with Kane. Recalled also the sensation of Kane's fingers stroking her cheek.

She'd wanted desperately to have him touch her, once. Now she almost wished that he had not. Ever since Kane touched her, distracting fancies had been fogging up her brain.

"Querida! Cuidado!" Pilar cried. Clea glanced up to see a man bearing down on her. He wore a workman's clothing, his features shadowed by his cap.

The stranger grabbed her arms. Clea tried to wrench away, but her feet tangled with her skirts, and she tripped instead.

Impossible to draw her little Spanish pistol, but she managed to elbow her assailant in his belly. He grunted but held her fast, dragging her toward a black-painted carriage.

Pedestrians stopped to stare. Clea dug in her heels. Pilar hastened after them, parasol in hand, calling out in Portuguese. The footman stood slack-jawed where she'd left him in the street.

"Socorro! Ligar à Polícia!" shrieked Pilar, as she brought her parasol down smartly on the villain's shoulders and head. He cursed again, released Clea, raised one arm to fend off Pilar's blows. Clea jerked away from him and ran, straight into the path of a heavy produce cart.

Four wheels, iron-rimmed. Two horses with yellowed teeth, sweating flanks, and white-rimmed eyes. A horrified driver, pulling back hard on the reins.

Clea closed her eyes.

Oh, Harry. How you would scold.

The impact, when it came, was not with wood or iron or horses' hooves, but human flesh and bone. Clea thudded to the ground several feet distant from the cart, and out of harm's way. "I am in your debt, sir," she gasped, when she had caught her breath. "Do you think you might let me up?"

Strong hands pulled her to her feet. Clea adjusted her bonnet, which had slid forward to rest on the bridge of her nose. Her gloves were torn, as was her skirt, her flesh rubbed raw from contact with the cobblestones. Amid the background hubbub of excited voices, she heard Pilar deploring, in passionate Portuguese, the tendency of the English to stand about and gape at dastardly deeds being enacted right in front of them without making the least effort to interfere.

Clea scanned the square. The black carriage had vanished. As had her accoster. As, for that matter, had the produce cart.

Clea returned her attention to her rescuer. Swarthy skin, prematurely grey hair, pale eyes—

Lisbon. Late 1810. "We meet again, Mr. Lawrence. The world is a small place."

"Your world nearly grew a great deal smaller, Lady Clea. I suggest we remove ourselves from the middle of the street." As he spoke, he took her arm.

"*Ao homen amado a fortuna lhe dá mão!*" exclaimed Pilar, as she hurried up to join them. "Fortune favors the bold. And you are very bold, eh, *hombre*? Such a gallant rescue. We owe you a debt of thanks."

The *hombre* glanced at Pilar, who was magnificently disheveled, her bosom heaving from her recent exertions. Appreciatively, he smiled. Clea said, with resignation, "Pilar, allow me to present Giles Lawrence. Giles, this is Senhora Estevez, who accompanied me here from Portugal."

Gallantly, Giles bowed. "*Prazer em conhecê-la,* Senhora Estevez."

Pilar dimpled. "The pleasure, Senhor Lawrence, is mine."

As they made sheep's eyes at one another, Clea dispatched her footman to fetch a pineapple-flavored ice for Pilar and a pistachio for Giles. For herself she chose a lemon sorbet.

The footman scurried off, corpse pale. She should have ordered *him* an ice. The poor man was having a difficult day.

Clea wasn't feeling quite the thing herself, being shaken from her near-kidnapping and bruised from her fall. When the footman rejoined them with the ices, she took her little pewter dish and limped toward the parcel-laden carriage. He trailed after her.

Giles Lawrence was the least likely of saviors, mused Clea. But perhaps the man had changed.

And perhaps pigs really could learn to fly.

All around her, people had resumed their conversations, as if nothing untoward had recently occurred, such as one of their number being well-nigh snatched off the street.

But Clea wasn't one of their number, was she? The *haut ton* found her almost as incomprehensible as the ragamuffin lounging against her brother's carriage, talking to his groom.

She narrowed her eyes. Clea had noticed that battered cap earlier, at the Ladies Bazaar. Its owner had snatched a toy windmill right out from under a stall keeper's nose.

Coincidence? Clea thought not. Since he was deep in conversation, her arrival was not noted by the groom. Nor by the ragged urchin, whose back was turned to her.

She grasped the collar of his shabby jacket. He swore and squirmed. Clea dropped the pewter dish and, with her other hand, took firm hold of his earlobe.

Not *his* earlobe, she realized. This waif wasn't a him but a her, and older than she first appeared.

"You've cobbled it," Clea informed her captive. "Tell me why you've been following me before I take my boot to your backside."

"Kiss me arse," replied the urchin, and kicked Clea viciously in her already bruised knee

Clea yelped and released both earlobe and collar. The ragamuffin snatched Clea's reticule from her wrist and disappeared into the crowd.

Chapter Eleven

The day is for honest men, the night for thieves. —
Euripides

Piccadilly was one of the busiest roads in London, a main thoroughfare since at least medieval times, home today to hotels and coaching inns, public houses and bars, St. James's Church.

Some of the more notable homes in London had once dominated the northern side of the street. Clarendon House was gone now, but Devonshire House and Burlington House remained. Next to Burlington House, separated from Piccadilly by a high wall and beyond it a courtyard, stood the Albany, a three-story mansion seven bays wide, with a pair of service wings flanking a front courtyard. First Melbourne and later York House prior to its incarnation as a hotel some eighteen years before, the Albany had become London's most prestigious bachelor address.

The hour was late when Kane arrived at his apartments, which included cellar and garret and kitchens in the attic, an anteroom with fireplace and a drawing room that opened by way of double doors into a bedroom with a dressing room behind. He permitted his valet to divest him of his boots and jacket and cravat, then sent the servant off to bed.

Lilah Kingston had provided a similar service, mere hours past. Kane wondered what it said about a man when his mistress interrupted an amorous encounter to inform him that repeated applications of white lead to the face would eventually paralyze the nerves. He returned to the drawing room and the decanter that waited on a richly grained mahogany sideboard.

A decanter that had much less brandy in it than when he'd seen it last.

A rustle of fabric, the scrape of leather soles against the wooden floor— Kane took firm hold of the decanter and swung round.

A cloaked figure emerged from the window enclosure. A female, he realized. This was hardly the first time a female had tried to breach his defenses. It *was* the first time one had gotten so far.

She pushed back the hood of her cloak. Mahogany curls. Bright green eyes. He said, "Clea! Are you mad?"

She held out an empty glass. *His* empty glass. "Do you mean to offer me refreshment, or bash me over the head?"

Feeling slightly foolish, Kane set down the decanter. "How did you get in?"

Somewhat unsteadily, Clea shrugged off her cloak. "I could shay — say! — I climbed the drainpipe, but the truth is that Julie taught me to pick locks. I snuck into the building when the doorman's attention was distracted elsewhere."

Kane's attention was distracted also, by a vision of Clea scrambling up a drainpipe clad in her dark gown and cloak, affording a glimpse of shapely ankles to anyone fortunate enough to be standing below.

He assumed her ankles were shapely. They had been shapely when she was a girl, and he saw no reason why they should be less so now. "Tell me you didn't come here unaccompanied. That you have a coachman waiting, or at the least a footman. Did you stop to consider the consequences, were you to be recognized?"

"I left my footman cooling his heels in a nearby tavern." As if to demonstrate the insalubrious effects of brandy upon a person's equilibrium, Clea plopped down uninvited onto a velvet-upholstered chair. She squinted at him. "When did you grow so careful of your reputation, Kane?"

"It's not *my* reputation that concerns me," he retorted, estimating how much of his brandy she'd consumed while awaiting his return. "Have you forgotten how dangerous London is after dark?"

"Danger is relative." Clea shifted position, causing a rearrangement of her skirts that revealed ankles every bit as shapely as he recalled. "It isn't in my nature to cower in a corner, Kane."

There were many kinds of danger, Kane might have told her, even for a young woman whose brother had once discovered her taking down the last messages of a dying British soldier seated on a wooden cot with his legs shattered and his head suspended from a sling attached to the wall. He elevated his gaze, found himself regarding the large carriage pistol that she held in one hand.

Clea regarded the weapon also, as if not altogether certain how it had come to be there. "I had a more practical weapon, but I lost it to a ragamuffin," she said. "In any event, Ned taught me to take care of myself a long time ago."

Ned should also have advised her not to hitch up her skirts in front of randy lechers. Kane's imaginings had advanced at an alarming pace from shapely ankles to carnal pleasures and illicit affairs.

The lapse was hardly surprising, he assured himself. He *was* alone with a young woman in his quarters in the dead of night.

The young woman seemed not the least bit perturbed that he was wearing merely shirt and trousers. Or interested, for that matter, which should have discouraged his imagination but, alas, did not.

Novel, to find himself deemed harmless. Kane didn't like it much.

He took Clea's weapon from her boneless hand, checked to see that it was loaded, set it prudently out of her reach. "Did it not occur to you that — how shall I phrase this politely? — I might not return home tonight?"

"That you might remain with your mistress? It is common knowledge that Baron Saxe almost always returns to his own bed. Rather, it *was* once common knowledge. I assumed your habits hadn't changed." Yawning, Clea arranged herself more comfortably in the chair.

Kane was glad that one of them was comfortable. He reclaimed the decanter and filled his glass.

When had he become so predictable? So dull?

"Yes, thank you, I would like some more brandy," announced Clea, from behind him. "Ignore me as you may, I'm not going to go away."

Harmless, predictable, and now he was being rude. Kane poured a generous splash of liquor into her empty glass. "Overlooking propriety, or impropriety, for the moment, why *are* you here?"

He handed Clea the glass. Her bare fingers brushed against his. Kane concluded that, when picking locks, a young woman must needs rid herself of the encumbrance of kid.

He wished she would put her gloves back on.

And then wished that she would not.

Clea squinted at him. "Have you set a street urchin to spying on me, Kane?"

Street urchin? Kane thought immediately of Pritchett, who had a pack of young miscreants at his disposal. But what interest might the Runner have in Clea? "I did not."

Clea took a swallow of her brandy, eyed her glass as if surprised to see that she still held it, set it aside and rose to her feet. Before Kane could step away from her — he *would* have stepped away from her, surely, had he had his wits about him — she slipped her arms around his neck. "I believe I may be inebriated," she said, and pressed her lips to his.

Inebriated? She was drunk as David's sow. Kane had not understood before that the condition was contagious. He felt more than a little intoxicated himself.

Lips and teeth and tongue. Murmured implorations and ragged breaths. His hands moved over Clea's slim torso, her fingers tugged at his hair ...

This wasn't the first time, either, that he had found himself the focus of feminine determination. However, never before had Kane's better nature been in such intense conflict with his worst.

Abruptly, he released Clea, uncertain whether he was more appalled by his behavior or hers.

She touched her fingers to her lips. "I dreamed of kithing — kissing! — you every night when I was fifteen."

At fifteen, Clea had been reading Ovid's *Art of Love*. Kane felt a tingle in his cheeks. The room was warm, he told himself. Rakehells didn't blush.

Nor, in the normal way of things, did rakehells' toes curl in their stockings as result of a simple embrace. He should immediately send Clea on her way.

At the very least, he should remove himself to the opposite side of the room.

Kane did neither, but remained where he was.

Clea hiccoughed. "According to Hannah and the gossips, you haven't a scruple to your name. Myself, I have decided you're not half so wicked as they claim."

Did she sound disappointed? Kane said, a trifle savagely, "In need of diversion, are you, brat? I might suggest a less dangerous pastime than housebreaking, in that case."

Clea looked around for the decanter, located it, splashed the remaining liquid in her glass. "Don't be a beef-wit."

Due to his penchant for both politics and philandering, Kane had been called many unflattering names. 'Beef-wit', however, had not previously been included in the list. "I repeat, why are you here?"

"I was accosted today. Outside Gunter's, in Berkeley Square." Clea steadied herself against the back of a chair.

Kane stared at her. "The deuce you say."

"Shall I show you my bruises?" Clea gestured with her glass. "I have enemies, Kane."

She was going to have the devil of head when the brandy wore off. "You're not going to tell me Mariel Marsden accosted you."

"I wouldn't put it past her, but no. The man had a damaged shoulder. Like the highwayman I shot."

"Hannah was right. You *should* have merely fainted," Kane remarked, far more calmly than he felt. "Revenge, do you suppose?"

"I don't know," admitted Clea. "Fortunately, Giles Lawrence was at hand. He snatched me from the jaws of danger. Or the wheels, in this case."

Kane had, in the course of his diplomatic dealings, developed a suspicious nature. Every instinct rejected the notion that Mr. Lawrence had taken himself to Berkeley Square in search of an ice. "I wasn't aware that you were acquainted." Giles hadn't mentioned that fact, damn the man.

Clea lifted her glass to her lips. "I am acquainted with a great many people. Most of them don't signify."

Kane took the glass from her, set it aside. She opened her eyes wider, putting him in mind of a tipsy owl. "I'm behaving badly, aren't I? But I'm growing very weary of villains popping out from behind the bushes and accosting me, Kane."

He slipped a cautious arm around her shoulders. Clea had survived England's hostilities with the French only to return to London and hostilities of another sort.

She huffed out a great sigh and leaned against him.

Kane inhaled the sweet smell of her hair.

Chapter Twelve

The sun shines also on the wicked. — Seneca

Mr. Pritchett of Bow Street was, due to the demands of his profession, perfectly at home in parts of London where his superiors dared not set foot. He was less at home in the East End, and more familiar than he liked with a certain establishment in King's Place.

The proprietress of said establishment regarded him ironically. "Here you are again, Mr. Pritchett. Hobnobbing with a harlot over the tea cups."

The Runner might have pointed out that he hadn't been offered tea, or brandy, or any of the other amenities of the establishment. This particular harlot was so far beyond his touch that she might have resided on the moon.

"Leave off, Lilah." Baron Saxe loosened his cravat. "Pritchett is about to tell us why he set one of his street brats to following Clea Fairchild."

Mrs. Kingston raised her eyebrows. "He did?"

"I didn't," protested Pritchett. "Which isn't to say that somebody else might not have."

"Somebody clearly has," retorted Kane. "I want to know why."

Pritchett reflected unhappily upon the fate of bearers of bad news. He hoped he would not have his head cut off for his pains.

Or his eyes and tongue cut out. "Word is that the Marsden family has hired Bow Street to nose out the facts about young Harry's death. Specifically, if Lady Clea might have been to blame."

" 'Word is'," echoed Mrs. Kingston. "You are not involved?"

Pritchett was not. While he had been occupied with a certain Shoreditch fencing ken, an encounter that resulted in him tumbling arse over teakettle down a staircase whilst gripping the proprietor by his leather apron, having the miscreant's knee driven hard into his groin and being set upon by the family bulldog, yet another plum assignment had gone elsewhere. "Townsend was requested." The Marsden family could afford to pay for the best.

"Maybe I will visit Australia," Kane muttered. He fixed Pritchett with a stern eye. "You will keep me informed. Now go away."

Pritchett could have informed Lord Saxe of many things, some of which Kane might have even liked to know. But he had been dismissed, and so he took his leave. In the street outside, he inhaled a deep breath of good, soot-laden, unperfumed air; then set out in search of sustenance and, more importantly, a pint.

Mere paces away from streets showcasing noble colonnades, bow windows and gleaming doorknockers, lay narrow lanes lined with gin shops, pawnbrokers, tenements and taverns left over from an earlier century. Pritchett followed a crooked path into the heart of the rookery, past broken-down buildings with cracked doors and rag-stuffed windows and gutters choked up with filth. He wove his way among thieves of every denomination, ragged children already steeped in every sort of vice, slatterns with bloated faces and vacant eyes.

In the heart of the rookery stood an ancient brick building known as Rat's Castle. Pritchett approached the door.

A gruff voice issued a challenge. He responded, heard the sound of a bolt being drawn back.

Were Pritchett a man devoted to his duty, he would be attempting to discover the source of the queer money currently exacerbating the Bank of England, not preparing to take his ease among bobtails and bullies, pickpockets and thieves.

A man's duty was one thing, his inclination another. The door swung open. The Runner stepped inside. Several paces down a hallway led him into a crowded common room.

Pritchett lowered his battered body onto a chair and ordered his drink. He had savored but a swallow before a pair of his fellow customers decided to have a turn-up, result of a certain Dimber Danny having insulted the current object of the other's affections, a slattern known as Billingsgate Moll. Cat's Meat Johnny took exception to the assertion that his lady was as well-worn as a barber chair in which an entire parish had sat to be trimmed.

"Shut yer bone box!" Cat's Meat Johnny demanded.

"Yer brains are in yer ballocks," Dimber Danny sneered. He was a handsome fellow. Cat's Meat Johnny was squat and snaggle-toothed, his features scarred by pox.

Cat's Meat Johnny planted his fist smack in the middle of Dimber Danny's face. Dimber Danny howled, and spat out a tooth, and delivered an uppercut to Cat's Meat Johnny's jaw. Spectators leapt up on chairs, tables, benches, energized by the sight of blood. This was no contest between two milling coves well-schooled in the noble art of self-defense but a rough-and-tumble ruction involving a great deal of sweat and shouting and splashing of blood, crunching of bone, bodies smashing into furniture and thudding to the floor.

Pritchett watched with idle interest. He was as fond of a bare-knuckle bout as the next man. It mattered not a whit to him that there were no umpires present to decide how to deal with such questionable practices as holding an opponent's hair to render him immobile while he was being pounded to a pulp. If Pritchett didn't lend his voice to a general conversation that contained such esoteric terms as 'muzzlers' and 'doublers', 'wisty cantors' and 'cross-and-jostle work' — and more enthusiastic comments such as 'crack his napper', 'mill his cannister', and 'bellows to mend' — he winced when appropriate, and occasionally cheered, and idly speculated whether he would see an ear bit clean through, or an eye gouged out.

Along with the other spectators, Pritchett had risen to his feet. Belatedly, he realized that someone had come up beside him, smelled the scent of a familiar soap.

Excitement fled and with it any pleasure he might have briefly felt.

"I hear," said the individual now standing next to him, "that you spoke with Baron Saxe today. About the brat who has been trailing after Clea Marsden, mayhap?"

This would teach him, Pritchett thought grimly, the folly of pretending for a moment that he was just an ordinary fellow observing a barroom brawl and enjoying a pint of ale. Had he not got caught up in the general excitement, he might have sensed the Deacon approaching and made his escape by means of the back door.

The sad truth about archvillains was that when one was tumbled off his perch, another swiftly climbed up to take his place.

Pritchett said, "I didn't set anyone on Lady Clea. And so I told his lordship."

"And did his lordship believe you?" the Deacon asked.

Pritchett doubted it. He wouldn't have believed himself, were he in the baron's shoes.

"I'm not sure that *I* believe you," said the Deacon, "the brat in question being young Frankie." He paused as the onlookers erupted, Cat's Meat Johnny having snatched up a stool and brought it down smartly on Dimber Dan's head.

Pritchett gathered up his wits. "Frankie's gone to ground," he muttered. "I've not seen her for several days."

The Deacon flicked open a silver snuffbox. "You've lost her, in other words."

Pritchett remained silent, contemplating the various reasons that Frankie might have hopped the twig.

The Deacon inhaled his snuff. Few men could sneeze in a menacing manner, but he managed to do exactly that.

Cat's Meat Johnny crashed to the floor, felled finally by a crushing blow delivered to the jugular with full force. The crowd howled and hissed, then, along with the combatants, applied themselves to the reviving effects of various alcoholic beverages.

"You are astonishingly ill-informed for a man of your profession," the Deacon observed. "Are you also unaware that Clea Marsden recently came close to being crushed under the wheels of a produce cart in Berkley Square?"

And wouldn't *that* have flung the fat into the fire?

In one swallow, Pritchett emptied his glass.

Chapter Thirteen

Question everything. Learn everything. Answer everything. — Euripides

Lady Clea was further flaunting her insouciance, and her excellent driving skills, on the leafy roadways of Hyde Park. Beside her in the graceful two-wheeled curricle, its lightweight body suspended from a pair of outsized swan-neck half-springs at the rear, sat Senhora Estevez. The curricle was large enough to accommodate its driver and one passenger, and drawn by a pair of perfectly matched bays.

"I do not mind placing myself in harm's way for a good cause," declared the senhora. "And I am devoted to you, furthermore. However, it will sorely strain our friendship if you dump me in a ditch."

Clea maneuvered the curricle around a cumbersome barouche. "You wound me. I have not overturned anyone yet." While it was true that curricles were notorious for the number of accidents in which they were involved, Hyde Park's byways at this fashionable hour were congested with superbly mounted gentlemen and ladies in dashing rigs. One did not move quickly through such a crush, but proceeded at a snail's pace.

"This is Rotten Row," she added. "Originally, the *route de roi*. William III caused three hundred oil lamps to be erected to light his way from Kensington Palace to St. James's, at the end of the seventeenth century. In those days, the park was a rutted haven for highwaymen."

"Highwaymen?" echoed Pilar, with a wary look around. "Have you forgot that each time someone has tried to interfere with you, it has been in a public setting such as this?"

Clea had forgotten nothing. Resting on the seat beside her, concealed in her reticule, lay a double barrel folding trigger pistol with a sliding hammer safety, its overall length six inches. Kane had sent the weapon, the morning after her visit to his rooms — in case, Clea supposed, she felt like shooting two people at the same time.

At the moment, she felt like shooting him.

She'd kissed Kane. He'd kissed her back. Before he recalled whom he was kissing and leapt back like a scalded cat. "Not each time," she said aloud. "You will recall the inn."

"*Certamente* I recall the inn," Pilar retorted. "We have already agreed that the intruder mistook my chamber for yours. Not that I mean to imply your bedchamber is a public place."

Public? Clea grimaced. So chaste was her bedchamber that she might have been a nun. A circumstance she'd not thought twice about until she'd drunk more brandy than she should, and flung herself at Kane.

She'd had an aching head the next day, and a large case of remorse. Did Kane let her within three feet of him again, she would apologize.

Kane would be accustomed to females flinging themselves at his feet.

Curse the man.

Clea nodded to an acquaintance. The woman didn't respond, her attention all for Senhora Estevez, who today was wearing a Spanish pelisse of shot sarsenet trimmed with Egyptian crape and antique cuffs with Chinese binding, a pink neck scarf with cherry stripes, a pale blue silk fringed parasol, lemon-colored kid slippers and gloves, and a Prussian helmet-shaped hat; and clutching a wicker cage from which frequently issued outraged yowls.

"Why is that woman staring at me?" Pilar asked.

"I can't imagine," Clea lied.

A faint plaintive chirrup issued from the cage. Pilar gave it a reassuring pat. "Do not fear, sweeting! I shall permit no one to steal you away from me. Even if a certain person refuses to see what is in front of her face."

Clea refrained from remarking that anyone who aspired to steal

Fausto must have windmills in his upper story. "I merely said that we shouldn't allow our imaginations to run riot," she protested.

"I am without imagination," Pilar responded. "You are the one who— *Droga!*" One of the bays had taken umbrage at a high-perch phaeton that was taking up more of the roadway than its fair share. Pilar clutched at Fausto's cage.

Expertly, Clea manipulated the reins. "You told me nothing was missing. Perhaps one of the maidservants sneaked a closer peek at your wardrobe."

"Speaking of one's wardrobe—" Pilar slid Clea a sly sideways glance. "Don't tell me you didn't take such care with your costume in hope that a certain baron might see you looking so well."

Pelisse of delicate fawn Irish poplin ornamented with white silk trim down the front and on the sleeves. Small cap of fawn velvet, tastefully edged with pearls, and a white ostrich feather which fell to the left side. Fawn slippers and gloves. Clea made no reply.

The sun was shining brightly. Ducks and geese and swans swam in the Serpentine, rabbits and squirrels rustled in the bushes, cows and deer grazed on the grass, birds twittered in the trees. The *ton* was also a-twitter, exchanging the latest on-dits, gossiping about the Queen's trial, speculating upon what circumstance had caused Clea Marsden to scowl like a thundercloud.

Pilar nudged her. "There is Senhor Lawrence. He is *muito* handsome, no?"

Mounted on a magnificent dappled gelding, Giles was riding toward them. Clea found the horse much more handsome than its rider. As Chaucer had put it, handsome is that handsome does.

"*Boa tarde, Senhor Lawrence.*" Pilar greeted Giles with a warm smile.

"A good afternoon to you, Senhora Estevaz. And to you, Lady Clea." Giles guided his horse to the far side of the curricle, the better to converse with Pilar.

Half-listening to their conversation, Clea scanned the crowd.

She saw no ruffian with a bandaged shoulder, no curly-haired ragamuffin, no — though she wasn't searching for him, not really — Baron Saxe.

A gaggle of gentlemen were riding toward the curricle. Clea recognized several of her husband's fellow officers. Jeremy Rossiter, fair and slender and aspiring toward dandyism, judging by the height of his shirt points. Feckless Freddy Thompson, who had a restless, nervous way about him, and whose pockets were perennially to let. Amiable Kit Graham.

A pang of sorrow struck her. Unsettling to encounter Harry's friends here, and in civilian attire.

Clea performed introductions. Giles hung back, looking bored.

Kit Graham urged his horse to her side. "It's good to see you, Lady Clea. I would have sought you out sooner, but I only recently arrived in town."

They passed a few moments in pleasant conversation, then Clea lowered her voice. "Can you help me, Kit? I'm trying to discover who Harry met in Lisbon shortly before he died."

He shifted uncomfortably in his saddle. "I believe Carruthers was in Portugal around that same time. You've heard he's come into the title, his sire having finally stuck his spoon in the wall?"

Clea had not. "Where might I find him?" she asked.

"In one fleshpot or another," Kit told her. "The poor devil is trying to drown his demons in a vat of gin."

"What demons?" Clea demanded.

"We all have demons. I'll make inquiries about Carruthers if you like. It was good to see you, Lady Clea." Kit turned his horse away.

Clea watched him disappear into the crowd. Not all the casualties of the Peninsular War lay in unmarked graves on foreign soil. Some returned home to struggle under familial responsibilities or alternately drink and drug themselves into oblivion.

The bays fidgeted, restive from having been kept standing so long. Clea took up her reins. Pilar waved a languid hand at her admirers as the carriage drew away.

Once Hyde Park had been part of a forest inhabited by wild boars and wolves, Clea advised her companion. Henry VIII had appropriated three hundred acres from the monks of Westminster to extend his hunting ground. Today the park was the hunting ground not only of the *beau monde,* set on seeing and being seen, but also of those lovely avaricious charmers known as Cyprians, or the Fashionably Impure.

One Cyprian in particular caught Clea's eye. She was wearing a habit of deep blue and a small beaver hat, and riding a pretty sorrel mare.

Who would know more about fleshpots than a procuress? Clea touched her whip to her horses' back.

The curricle leapt forward. Pilar clutched at the wicker cage. "*Pelo amor de Deus!* What are you doing? Who is that?"

Clea maneuvered her curricle around a landeau. "*That* is a Paphian. Baron Saxe's favorite Paphian, to be precise." She drew up beside the sorrel mare. "Mrs. Kingston. A word, if you will."

The lavender eyes coolly appraised her. "You have very much the look of your brother, Lady Clea. He would hardly approve of us meeting like this."

Nor would Kane, reflected Clea. "I accompanied my brother to the Peninsula. You are hardly the first fallen woman whose path mine has crossed."

"Nor, I daresay, will I be the last," Mrs. Kingston responded wryly. "What is it you wish to speak to me about?"

Kane would have embraced this woman countless times. Clea wanted to box her ears. "I believe you may be acquainted with Viscount Carruthers," she said.

Mrs. Kingston raised her eyebrows. "There are very few young gentlemen in London that I am *not* acquainted with. It is a rite of passage if you will."

"*Querida,*" Pilar murmured. "You are attracting much attention."

Clea glanced over her shoulder. Giles Lawrence was riding toward them, looking cross.

Mrs. Kingston gathered up her reins.

Chapter Fourteen

I am bound to tell what I am told, but not in every case to believe it. — Herodotus

Lord Saxe rode his great black Arabian stallion through the fine Portland stone archway of Temple Bar, where the Strand became Fleet Street, and atop which the heads of executed traitors had been exhibited until late in the previous century. Zeus pulled on the reins and snorted, displaying his dislike of this noisy, noisome part of town.

Kane shared his steed's ill-temper. He was in a thoroughly sour mood. Henry Brougham, Princess Caroline's Attorney-General, a brilliant lawyer and leading Whig politician, was taking every advantage of his position at center stage. Kane had spent the past two days sitting through Brougham's opening speech in the Queen's defense.

He was awed by his knowledge of his client's innocence, Brougham had announced, and warned the peers against bringing about a country-wide cataclysm on the basis of flimsy evidence. He had more than sufficient facts at his disposal, he said, to make a charge of recrimination against the King, thereby providing his client the opportunity to argue that her husband's behavior had been as bad as, if not worse than, hers; but he would not produce this inflammatory material unless he must. In the final analysis his duty must be to his client, and let the consequences fall as they may.

It had been a magnificent speech. Bets were being taken at Brooks's club that the Bill would be thrown out.

Magnificent speech or no, Prinny had lost none of his appetite for divorce.

As Castlereagh had put it, "We are in a pretty mess."

Wakely Court loomed up ahead. Embellished by a succession of indulgent owners with an exuberance of arches and gables, turrets and a forest of tall rectangular chimneys, the eccentric structure stretched three stories above the street.

Kane dismounted, passed his reins to a waiting groom. Zeus bared large, yellowed teeth. " 'ere now, we'll have none o' yer tomfoolery," the groom scolded the horse.

Tidcombe opened the front door. "Good afternoon, my lord. Lord Dorset is in the schoolroom."

"I'll find my own way." Kane handed the butler his tall curly-brimmed beaver hat and gloves, and mounted the stair.

The door to the schoolroom stood open. Kane paused on the threshold.

Diamond-shaped windows sat high in plastered walls that bore traces of faded murals painted in once-brilliant reds and blues and greens. Scattered around the scarred wooden floor were wainscot benches, tables and chests. Seated in a massive oak box chair was a singularly attractive man with dark auburn hair and clear green eyes, his face saved from being beautiful by a slightly aquiline nose. The fifteenth Earl of Dorset was dressed for travel in a brown single-breasted riding coat, buckskin breeches and tall, dusty boots. He was leafing through *A Greene Forest, or a Naturall Historie,* written by one John Maplet in 1567.

Kane closed the door behind him. Ned glanced up from his book. "Here I am, at your command. What is this mysterious 'urgent matter' that necessitates my return to town?"

"I'm surprised you didn't come back immediately you learned Clea was in residence." Kane strolled around the chamber, past a counting table with a checkered top. "Why are we in the schoolroom? Are you reliving your salad days?"

Ned closed his book, set it aside. "Old habits die hard. Here, we are unlikely to be overheard. By the bye, Julie says that you're not to involve me in any of Castlereagh's intrigues."

Kane, who viewed the current countess with the suspicion of a mostly law-abiding citizen for an allegedly reformed criminal, responded noncommittally, "I hope that she is well."

"Fit as a fiddle, save for a tendency toward dyspepsia," fondly replied the Earl, who was so unfashionable as to be besotted with his wife. "I was reluctant to leave her in Sussex but she promised she'd not set the household at sixes and sevens again until after I return. I repeat, what is so urgent? I meant what I told you when we left Town. I won't have Castlereagh involving Julie in this current imbroglio."

Kane could hardly blame Ned for disliking the prospect of his wife scampering over rooftops and down drainpipes, spying on the Queen. "Your Julie survived worse than Castlereagh before you removed her from the streets."

"Diplomatic as ever, I see," Ned said wryly. "Some things never change."

Kane did not care to discuss his diplomacy or the lack thereof. "You haven't seen Clea yet?"

"My sister was out when I arrived. Clea wrote that she had brought Pilar home with her. I daresay they're cutting up some lark."

A lark? Surely it was more than that?

Or maybe it was not. "When I returned to the Albany two nights ago, Clea was waiting for me there."

The earl looked mildly interested. "Why would she do that?"

Ned saw no obvious reason why his sister might visit a notorious degenerate's chambers? Kane found himself annoyed. He didn't care to have his friend to think the worst of him, of course, but—

Clea had kissed him, which she damned well shouldn't have. For that matter, he damned well shouldn't have either, but that was beside the point.

True, she'd had too much to drink.

Did she need to be half-drunk to want to kiss him?

Aargh.

Kane said, "You might make some effort to keep your sister under control."

"And I might spare myself the trouble," Ned responded. "Permit me to remind you that Clea has had several birthdays since you last met. She is one-and-twenty, and must know her own business best."

How was it Kane hadn't realized before that the Fairchilds were not entirely of sound mind? "If it were to get out round that Clea visited my rooms—"

"Cousin Hannah would wash her hands of us," Ned responded cheerfully. "One can only hope."

Ned had decided he was making a great piece of work about nothing? Kane gritted his teeth.

"Clea generally has an explanation for the seemingly outrageous things she does," Ned added. "I confess to being curious as to what her reason was this time."

Kane doubted his old friend would remain so nonchalant were he to be enlightened regarding schoolgirl passions and Ovid-inspired dreams. Most likely, Ned would cut out Kane's liver and fry it for breakfast, as well he should. "I understand you are acquainted with Giles Lawrence," he said.

"I am. Why do you ask?"

"Giles Lawrence recently saved Clea from being crushed under the wheels of a produce cart."

By the time Kane finished recounting Clea's misadventures in Berkeley Square, her brother's nonchalance had vanished. Kane concluded, "Giles claims he just happened to be present. I don't believe him, of course."

"Of course you don't," said Ned. "But sometimes a coincidence is just that."

"More often," Kane reminded him, "it's not. As you know very well."

The earl was briefly silent, lost in contemplation of one dusty boot. Kane took another turn around the room. Some long-forgot Fairchild ancestor had had an eclectic education. On the shelves, shoulder to shoulder with classical Greek and Latin scholars, were Samuel Richardson, Daniel Defoe, Jonathan Swift. "Clea accused me of having her followed. I in turn accused Pritchett, who claims to be innocent as a newborn babe. This leads me to conclude that Pritchett either knows nothing of the matter, or that he is more wary of someone else than he is of me. *Or* that he has been handsomely reimbursed."

"But reimbursed by whom?" asked Ned.

"And why? Mariel Marsden has hired a Runner — not Pritchett, which clearly rankles. Clea says the man who tried to abduct her resembled the highwayman she shot." Kane observed his friend's startled expression. "I mentioned that your sister shot a highwayman, did I not?"

"I was hoping this would prove to be a farrago of nonsense," Ned sighed. "Julie will demand to come to London so that she may stick her finger in the pie."

"Don't tell her," Kane advised.

"A man doesn't lie to his wife."

Kane snorted at the absurdity of this remark. Ruefully, Ned smiled. "Or I don't, at any rate. How much has Clea told you about her husband, Kane?"

Enough that Kane had developed an antipathy for Harry Marsden, no matter that he'd barely known the man. "What makes you think she told me anything?"

"You've been dandling Clea on your knee since was an infant," Ned retorted. "Granted, that is an absurd reason for trusting you, but she always has."

At the notion of Clea on his knee — on *her* knees — Kane felt his pulse kick up several beats. "The official verdict is that Marsden accidentally shot himself. Clea believes otherwise."

Ned reached for the abacus. With an idle finger, he rearranged the beads. "Clea may be correct. Harry Marsden was up to his ears in some secret business for Wellington. That information, you understand, must remain between ourselves."

Chapter Fifteen

Every man is like the company he is wont to keep. —
Euripides

When Clea returned to Wakely Court, Tidcombe was waiting by the front door. "Lord Dorset would like to speak with you at your earliest convenience, my lady. In the library." The butler bowed stiffly, then took himself off to the nether regions of the house.

"Ned, here!" Pilar marveled. "Shall Fausto and I accompany you into the lion's den?"

Clea made her way to her bedchamber. "Thank you, but no."

Moments later, she walked into the library. Her brother was seated at the desk.

A fire burned merrily in the hearth. Tidcombe had seen to his master's comfort. Or, more likely, Ned had built the fire himself.

She closed the door behind her, crossed the drafty floor. "Hallo, Ned. Has someone has been telling tales?"

"Someone was bound to, eventually." He studied her. "What devilment have you been up to, puss?"

Clea placed a pistol on the cluttered desk. "What do you make of this?"

"French," he responded promptly. "A fairly unremarkable Maubeuge .69 gauge flintlock, brass mounted with a walnut stock and a brass frame. Manufactured by the main French arsenal, primarily for cavalry use." He inspected the left side of the barrel. "Dated 1813. Incidentally, welcome home."

"I'm glad to see you, too." Clea set a second gun on the desk by the first. "And this?"

"An officer's pistol, made by Mr. Manton: a part-round 62 caliber octagon barrel with a silver band inlaid at the breech, straight grain European walnut stock, rectangular silver thumb-grip. The barrel flats and tangs are decorated with foliate engraving and the hammer spurs with stylized sea serpents; the iron trigger guard has engraved pineapple-shaped finials." Ned placed the weapon beside the other on the desk. "And you know as well as I that it is one of a pair."

"Harry had the matching pistol with him when he left our lodgings that last night." Clea indicated the first gun. "Yet this was discovered by his body, and Harry's pistol was nowhere to be found. His murderer must have exchanged the weapons. I'd never seen this gun before that night."

Ned studied the two pistols. "You said nothing at the time?"

"I tried. No one cared to listen. Pilar suggested I would do better to keep my reservations to myself. One has a better chance of flushing out a fox, she tells me, if the fox is unaware the hounds have caught his scent."

Ned looked pensive. He, at least, was not inclined to disbelieve her, Clea thought. Unlike the Portuguese officials who had dismissed her protests as the ravings of a grief-stricken wife.

Nor did Ned seem surprised. Although, she conceded, it would take a great deal to unsettle a man who had spied his way through the Peninsular War, most often behind enemy lines, learning troop movements and gathering strategic information, risking constant exposure and death. Clea was reminded of the little notebook that had been buried in Harry's trunk.

In an attempt to keep her occupied while they were in the Peninsula, Ned had set her to studying codes under the skeptical eye of George Scoville, whose Army Guides were attempting to decipher intercepted French communications. Major Scoville had gone on to crack the Army of Portugal code, and the Great Paris Code the following year. Clea had merely progressed to the point that she could recognize a cipher key when one bit her on the nose.

How had Harry come to have a stranger's notebook in his possession? Until she knew the answer to that question, she would keep the fact of its existence to herself.

Clea told her brother, instead, about her mother-in-law's accusations. She *didn't* tell him that she'd drunk more brandy than she should have and kissed his closest friend. "Mariel is informing all of the world that I am not a proper sort of female. She may have a point."

Ned leaned back in his chair and propped his boots up on the desk. " 'Proper' is hardly a word ordinarily associated with the Fairchilds. But for the sake of argument: How so?"

Clea gazed down at the desk. "I can't help but wonder what might have happened — or might *not* have happened — if I had tried to prevent Harry from going out that night. But I was weary of his moods, and took a few moments for myself."

" 'A thousand regrets do not cancel one debt'," Ned murmured. "While it is common enough to question oneself after a tragic event, it is also a waste of time. You were precisely the sort of wife Harry wanted, my girl, or he wouldn't have braved my wrath to marry you."

Absurdly close to tears, Clea closed her hands into fists. "Mariel is right about one thing. Harry *was* too familiar with firearms to have accidentally shot himself."

Ned picked up the strange pistol. "It will have occurred to you, I trust, that ruffians do not commonly try to abduct young women in the middle of Berkeley Square."

Clea bit her lip. Kane had told him of the incident, no doubt. What else might Kane have said?

The library door opened. Pilar entered, holding Fausto in her arms. The cat's blue-grey coat was ruffled, his golden eyes slitted, his tail moving back and forth like the pendulum of a clock.

Ned stood to greet her. "*Bom te ver,* Pilar."

Pilar set Fausto on the floor. "It is nice to see you also, *caro.* Lord Saxe summoned you to London? *Muito macho,* that one. Or should I say *gato macho*? With such a man, one must remind oneself that at night all cats are grey." A footman followed her into the room, carrying a tray laden with a teapot and cups, sugar bowl and tongs and milk jug, and a plate piled high with pastries.

The footman deposited the heavy tray on the desk. The senhora thanked him prettily, bade him begone, and set about efficiently preparing tea.

Clea selected a little cake studded with fruit and flavored with rosewater and almonds; leaned against the desk and attempted not to spill crumbs down the front of her dress.

Fausto vanished behind a stack of books.

Pilar presented Ned with tea, and Clea; helped herself to a large bun, with butter. "And so! Such adventures we have had. Has Clea told you there have been six or seven attempts to interfere with her? I do not suggest 'interfere' in any pleasurable sense, you understand."

Ned looked up from the pastry tray. "Clea has not."

Pilar explained, a trifle indistinctly, about Clea's various near-mishaps. "That makes only six," said Ned, at her conclusion.

"I have in hindsight grown suspicious of a robbery that occurred at the inn where Clea was staying." Pilar pushed some papers aside and hitched herself up on the desk.

Ned turned to his sister. "When did this robbery take place, puss?"

Clea swallowed a mouthful of cake before she spoke. "Shortly after Harry's death. A number of rooms were broken into and various small items taken. Shortly after that, I took refuge with Pilar."

A scratch came at the door. It opened. "The Dowager Countess of Dorset," Tidcombe announced.

"For our sins," Ned muttered. "Show her in."

Tidcombe withdrew.

The dowager appeared in the doorway. Upon glimpsing the trio grouped cozily around — and on — the desk, she stopped in her tracks. "You, here, Fairchild? When did you arrive? Why are the three of you lounging about like Bacchants?"

"What is this Bacchant?" inquired Pilar.

"Cousin Hannah doesn't deem it proper," Clea explained, "for you to be sitting on the desk. Or for me to be leaning against it, I daresay."

The dowager's disapproving gaze shifted from her cousins to the pistols lying on the desk. "I'll tell you what's improper. 'Tis this affinity you have for weapons. It is something else for which we may blame the French."

Pilar rolled her eyes. "*Bom dia*, Lady Dorset. Would you care for tea?"

"No, I would not!" Hannah snapped. "You should lock your sister up somewhere, Fairchild, and throw away the key. Bad enough that she made a spectacle of herself outside Gunter's, but now she has been seen speaking with a bird of paradise in Hyde Park. She will never catch another husband at this rate."

Ned, who had risen again on his cousin's arrival, remained standing while she arranged herself in an ancient carved oak chair. "Do you want another husband, puss?"

"I do not."

Pilar eyed the pastry tray. "Why is it so shocking that one should speak with a bird? Me, I talk to my cat. He does not answer, but it pleases me all the same."

Hannah replied, impatiently, "Not *that* sort of bird. A barque of frailty. A prime article of virtue. Lilah Kingston, specifically."

"Ah! A *prostituta*." Pilar selected a seed cake. "Conversation would go on much smoother if you English could be brought to say outright what you mean."

"The female in point isn't a mere prostitute but the overseer of a house of assignation," Ned remarked. "Come down out of the boughs, Hannah. My sister has seen a great deal more of the world than you have, and furthermore is of an age to speak to whomever she may please."

"*De facto!*" said Signora Estevez. "You know this non-*prostituta*, Ned?"

"I *knew* her," Ned amended. "We have not spoken in some time. At the termination of our, ah, association, I made her a present of the house in King's Place. Mrs. Kingston had recently rescued Julie from a somewhat less respectable establishment. One might almost consider her an old friend of the family."

The dowager opened her mouth and closed it, rather like a dying fish.

Fausto, while the humans thus observed the social niceties, had amused himself first with the calculating board and counters, and after that the perpetual almanac in its frame; had rearranged various items on the mantle to his satisfaction and while so doing dispensed with a few, all the while keeping an eye out in case a reckless rodent ventured from its nest.

At last his patience was rewarded. Gleefully, he pounced. Sounds of scuffle; frantic squeaks; a stack of books toppled over with a thud. Fausto emerged triumphant from the disorder, a fat gray mouse dangling limply from his jaw.

He deposited his trophy at Pilar's feet. "What a clever boy you are," the senhora crooned. With one of her pretty kid slippers, she nudged the furry corpse out of sight under her chair.

"Gad!" ejaculated the dowager. "Rodents. What next?"

"Fausto is a great hunter," Pilar said reprovingly. "Very fast, very brave. His ancestors were feral mountain cats brought back to France by knights returning from the Crusades."

Under cover of this conversation, Clea leaned closer to Ned. "I wanted to ask Mrs. Kingston if she was acquainted with Viscount Carruthers. Kit Graham told me Clive was also in Portugal when Harry died."

"Forget Carruthers." Ned poured tea into her empty cup. "Ask Kane to secure you an audience with Wellington. At the least, it will provide him with something to think about other than the Queen's trial."

Chapter Sixteen

It better befits a man to laugh at life than to lament over it. — Seneca

Lord Saxe, in those same moments, was engaged in an intimate audience of his own. Mrs. Kingston having taken umbrage at his suggestion that she shouldn't speak to whomever she wished when out about the town, and then becoming additionally annoyed by his inquiry as to whether she'd numbered Harry Marsden among her young gentlemen acquaintances, it took the baron's vast persuasive powers, plus the gift of an exceptionally fine porcelain Harlequin figurine, to persuade her to come down out of the boughs.

Not caring to part on bad terms with his mistress, Kane consequently lingered longer at the Academy than he had planned; and if he managed to refrain from engaging in Bacchic revelries — this coming evening's *pièce de résistance* was to be a Roman *orgia*, complete with torch-lit saturnalian masked dances, followed by a supper of *rôti de boeuf* and green peas to build up the participants' stamina, washed down with some excellent claret to fortify their blood — he still imbibed a great deal more brandy than was wise, which resulted in him plunging his head into a bucket of cold water to try and clear the cobwebs from his brain. After he finally departed King's Place he called at Wakely Court, only to be told that Ned had left for Sussex, and Clea for Almack's. *Why* Clea decided to present herself at such a place had Pilar in a puzzle, that lady confessed; to Pilar, an evening spent dancing to insipid music and refreshing oneself with lemonade and stale cake sounded deadly dull.

It was just as well Clea wasn't at home. Kane hadn't yet determined whether he wanted more to toss up her skirts or shake her until her teeth rattled in her head.

The clock had already struck the quarter hour when he arrived at Almack's Assembly Rooms. Three-quarters of the nobility were not privileged to set foot inside this exclusive temple of the *ton*, and none were admitted after eleven o'clock.

Including, on a memorable occasion, the Duke of Wellington.

Kane mounted the grand staircase that led to the ballroom, causing several of his fellow guests to conjecture why a notorious Lothario would choose so sedate an evening's entertainment when he might more merrily amuse himself within less hallowed halls and in much livelier company, and others to conclude that the Lady Patronesses were no less susceptible than the general female population to this particular Lothario's practiced charm.

He entered the ballroom, one hundred feet long and almost half as wide, which was decorated with gilt columns and pilasters, classic medallions, mirrors that reflected countless lighted wax candles with bedazzling effect. Around the perimeters ranged sofas, one at the upper end of the room reserved for the exclusive use of the Lady Patronesses. Crimson silken ropes marked off the dance floor, crowded now with young ladies dressed in chaste white and gentlemen in knee-breeches, excellently fitting coats of superfine, and pristine cravats. Garlands of flowers adorned the space occupied by the orchestra.

A sharp-eyed, dark-haired woman approached him. "Saxe. You flatter us with your presence," she said.

Kane bent over her hand. "By noticing my presence, Dorothea, you flatter me instead."

"Palaverer," she replied appreciatively. "We've seen little of you of late. How boring London will be when the Queen's trial has ended! But you will not speak of such things to me." She gave him an arch look.

"I expect you know as much as I do about the current proceedings," Kane responded. Countess Lieven was the wife of the Russian ambassador. "If not more."

"I know that Brougham is edging dangerously close to sedition," she said. "And that Sidmouth and Castlereagh have a standing wager on which of them is the most unpopular man in England on any given day." She nodded toward the dance floor, where a quadrille was ending. "Warn Lady Clea to take care how she makes mischief. She would not have to find her voucher revoked."

In other words, whatever rumors Mariel Marsden might put about, Clea remained a favorite with the Patronesses, up to the point of outright scandal, which they would not tolerate.

Kane concluded that Dorothea Lieven had not yet heard about Clea's recent encounter with the notorious Mrs. Kingston. He thanked her for her forbearance, and made his way through the crowd.

Clea stood on the sidelines, surrounded by several of her husband's friends. Dandy Rossiter was taking care not to turn his head too quickly lest he cut his throat on his stiffly starched shirt-points. Kit Graham looked preoccupied. Freddy Thompson, come to try his luck with the latest entries in the matrimonial sweepstakes, was ogling Clea's clinging gown of ecru crepe de chine, which had puffed sleeves cut low and off her shoulders, a skirt elaborately trimmed with blonde lace, and a bodice plunging halfway to her waist. Emeralds circled her slender throat and dangled from her ears, sparkled in her hair.

Kane was suddenly as sober as a stone.

He'd managed to avoid Clea since the night when she'd come uninvited to his rooms. Had managed not to think about her for as long as an hour at a time, only to have her dance through his dreams when he finally fell asleep.

Kane enjoyed those dreams immensely.

He really was most damnably depraved.

She saw him, broke off her conversation and moved purposefully toward him. The expression on her lovely face suggested that she might like to box his ears.

" 'In childhood be modest,' " she quoted, as she reached his side. " 'In youth temperate, in adulthood just, and in old age prudent'. Socrates."

Kane hoped he was just. Prudence was beyond him at this point. "I am hardly as old as Methuselah," he protested.

Clea glowered at him. "No, but you are grown as dull. I've you to thank, I take it, for tattling on me to Ned."

Kane conceded that Clea had some cause for her annoyance. "You have put yourself in danger. Of course I informed Ned. Though I might sometimes be tempted to throttle you, I would not want anyone else to harm you, brat. I had your best interests in mind."

Hadn't he?

Or had he hoped Ned would play chaperone?

Clea mulled this over for a minute. "I owe you an apology. The other night, I shouldn't have—"

"No, you shouldn't," Kane interrupted. "And neither should I. Therefore we won't speak of it again. Dorothea Lieven bade me convey a warning. You are not to make a scandal, she says."

Clea flicked open the fan that dangled alongside her reticule at her wrist, a delicate confection of bone and silk and lace. "Does that mean I am to refrain from invading gentlemen's lodgings?" she asked, with a flirtatious sideways glance.

Kane experienced a queer clutching sensation in his gut. Dyspepsia, he told himself. He would not, absolutely could not, speculate upon how many gentlemen's lodgings Clea might have visited, or what she might have done once there. "I hope Dorothea meant nothing so specific. Nonetheless, it is good advice. While I declined your, ah, invitation, some other man might not."

"I might not want him to." Clea eyed him over the rim of her fan. "Why *did* you rebuff me? I should not say so, but I am hardly a hag. And you are hardly a model of restraint."

Why had he rebuffed her? For an instant, Kane could not recall.

He pinched himself. "Because I am your brother's friend. Because you are one-and-twenty and I am almost twice your age."

"Because you are a libertine and are loathe to tarnish my innocence. Or what is left of it." She grinned.

This was a highly improper conversation to be having anywhere, let alone at Almack's. Kane was enjoying it far more than he should. "An innocent wouldn't have worn that gown."

Clea snapped her fan shut. "Under other circumstances, I might appreciate the irony of being lectured on propriety by a philanderer. When did you become such a prude?"

First he was a beef-wit, now a prude? "You may call me whatever you wish. The fact remains that, if you are determined to be debauched, you would be far better suited by someone nearer your age."

Clea shrugged, an act that did interesting things to her neckline. "Few people my age have seen a man blown in half by a cannon ball."

"Nor have I," Kane pointed out. "Have you so little care for your safety that you would go about unarmed?"

She lowered her lashes. "Why should you assume that I'm unarmed?"

Kane's imagination ran riot. Where might Clea have hidden something under that scrap of a dress?

She added, teasingly, "If you are unaware of how a lady's fan may be used as a weapon, you're not half as experienced as I once believed."

Kane made no reply. If Clea had set out to provoke him, she was succeeding very well.

The band struck up a waltz, that shocking excuse for hugging and squeezing first introduced to Almack's by Countess Lieven and 'Cupid' Palmerston. Without asking permission, Kane grasped Clea's hand and led her out onto the floor.

"I considered procuring a visitor's ticket for Pilar," she remarked, as they promenaded side by side. "She would find Almack's an amusing study in English mating rituals. But then I realized Pilar would probably inform the Lady Patronesses that she had been the mistress of a Portuguese *bandido*, and decided I would not. You see, I can behave with proper prudence when the occasion demands."

Kane only hoped that he might do so. "Do you find Almack's an amusing study in English manners? Is that why you're here? I do not recall that such stuff was ever to your taste."

She stepped easily into his embrace, resting her left hand on his shoulder as he clasped her right. "Perhaps I've changed."

Repressing an impulse to draw her closer than was proper, Kane swept her whirling down the floor. "Not as much as that, I think. Senhora Estevez told me that Ned has left town."

"He went to fetch his wife. Cousin Hannah is under the delusion that Julie will make me toe the mark." Clea's hand tightened on his shoulder. "If you've come to scold me for speaking to your mistress, you may save your breath."

Kane contemplated the sort of things Lilah might discuss with an inquisitive young widow. The Suspended Scissors, for example. Or The Fixing of a Nail.

"Erm," he said.

Clea frowned. "If you must know, I am trying to locate Clive Carruthers, and hoped Mrs. Kingston might know his whereabouts. I was told he, ah, frequents establishments such as hers. And before you ask me *why,* pray recall that I am trying to discover why my husband got himself shot. Kit Graham told me that Carruthers also returned to Portugal."

Kane whirled Clea faster and faster around the dance floor. Maybe if he spun her silly, she might be made more susceptible to common sense.

Why Carruthers? he asked himself. What could the viscount know — or if he knew remember, being as the drunken sot appeared determined to piss away his inheritance with whores and games of chance? And what in Hades was so important about Portugal? Lest *he* grow giddy and disoriented, Kane slowed his steps.

"Ned told me I should forget speaking with Carruthers and ask you to arrange an audience with Wellington instead," Clea added, a trifle breathlessly.

To the ever-growing list of people he would like to throttle, Kane added his old friend Ned. "Talking to Wellington is like eavesdropping," he told Clea. "You may not like what you hear. Too, it would be better to keep the duke in reserve, unless you want to reveal your hand. There'll be no secrets kept once he becomes involved."

Clea's eyes fixed on his face. "What secrets? What do you know that I do not?"

Had it been another woman who fit so sweetly in his arms, Kane might have offered to advance her education. But since it was Clea—

Hemlock, applied to the privy parts, stops lustful thoughts.

"Did you not just say that old age should bring prudence? Humor me," Kane snapped.

Chapter Seventeen

Tell me, how does it feel with my teeth in your heart? —
Euripides

The hour was late, the night air chill. Tendrils of ghostly fog twined around the inadequate streetlights.

Covent Garden market was closed, the stalls shuttered. An ancient watchman with his lantern cried out the hour. In some nearby street, a night coach's wheels clattered over cobblestones.

In a previous century, many a brothel had lurked behind these fine old facades. The windows opening onto the Piazza had been lined with whores from seven at night until five the following morn.

If Covent Garden was no longer the haven of vice it once had been, neither was it the meeting place of saints. Reckless young lordlings still wagered entire fortunes in establishments where wiser men hesitated to set foot. Children of the streets still slipped their hands into careless pockets, and weren't they growing younger every day? Prostitutes of both sexes still hawked their wares.

The rooms abovestairs in the Three Pigeons were still hired out to good use.

The Deacon cast barely a glance into the taproom, or the chamber where a posture woman was entertaining her audience; he wasn't tempted even by the cellar where a rat-baiting was underway.

The current record was held by a fox terrier who slew a hundred rats in fifteen minutes.

The Deacon doubted that record would be broke tonight.

He mounted the stair.

The upper hallway was dark, dingy, dungeon-like, bare of any furniture, lined with closed doors. Leaning against the wall was a thick-set balding bruiser with misshapen ears and a flattened nose. On glimpsing the Deacon, he straightened to his full height.

If he'd had a forelock, he'd have tugged it. The Deacon held out a hand. The bruiser dropped a key onto his palm then slunk down the stairs, there to rot his guts with Strip-Me-Naked, or goggle at the posture woman, or hire himself a whore.

Whores there were a plenty in this place, some willing and some not. Could the walls talk, they might tell of the twelve-year-old girl fresh from the country, for instance, who'd been picked up by a kindly lady with the promise of employment as a maid. The kindly lady had brought her here instead, where she'd been drugged and sold to a randy merchant. He'd paid thirteen pounds for her first use.

It was a common enough practice. A pinch of snuff in a lass's beer would keep her quiet while the laddies had their way.

That country girl was still here, hiking up her skirts in some dark dirty corner for a great deal less than thirteen pounds.

The Deacon inserted the key into its lock. The room beyond had thick plaster walls and a double carpet on the floor, windows secured with both heavy curtains and shutters. Did a girl scream till she was hoarse, not a sound would be heard in the rooms below.

The door swung inward. The room was dimly candle-lit. As he entered, a woman rose from the bed. Coppery curls, green eyes, a lissome figure — she bore a startling resemblance to Clea Marsden, who was leading the Deaco such a merry dance.

He could have snatched Lady Clea when she snuck out to Saxe's rooms, *would* have snatched her had he been apprised of her nocturnal wanderings in time, which he hadn't been, for which someone had paid dear.

Next Lady Clea had accosted Lilah Kingston. Her protectors might be forcing the Deacon to keep a prudent distance, but they weren't doing a very good job of keeping her ladyship from doing foolish things.

Eventually, she would make a misstep that worked to his advantage.

The Deacon's patience was wearing thin.

" 'ere now, 'andsome, what's your liking? Bread and butter, French, Greek style?" The woman sauntered toward him, suggesting that she might fiddle with his jiggling bone. Give him a tongue job. Or, if it was to his liking, he might explore her pleasure-pot firsthand.

"Silence!" So easily, the illusion of Clea was destroyed. The Deacon caught the whore's arm and wrenched it behind her back.

Her eyes flew to his face. So close, she could not help but recognize him, despite his wig and paint. Blanching, she tried to twist away.

The Deacon glanced around the room, found the birch rod left where he'd instructed.

He grasped the whip and raised it, then brought it down, hard.

Chapter Eighteen

Nothing is to be preferred before justice. — Socrates

What secrets? wondered Clea. What secrets did Kane know?

All manner, she imagined. Secrets of an erotic nature that Mrs. Kingston doubtless shared.

Clea had not expected that Kane's mistress would be a painted harlot. Nor had she expected that Lilah Kingston would be one of the most attractive females she had ever seen.

Kane would not have been so eager to show Mrs. Kingston the door had he found *her* waiting in his rooms.

'Use the occasion for it passes swiftly'. Ovid. Clea had used the occasion, and what had it gotten her? A brief moment of intense pleasure followed by even more intense frustration. She consoled herself that Kane had sufficiently forgot himself to kiss her, really kiss her, for a moment.

And she'd not recovered from it yet.

She'd shocked him, she decided. They wouldn't speak of it, he said. The man had misbehaved with at least half the females in London, but he couldn't bring himself to misbehave with her.

He thought she was an innocent, and in some ways Clea was. But if she were to be debauched, the thing would not be better done by someone nearer her own age.

Tempted to throttle her, was he? Clea was tempted to throttle *him*.

She couldn't help but recall how well they'd waltzed together. Which led her to imagine that Kane might engage with her in other matters equally well.

Since she managed to either assault him or insult him every time they met, she wasn't likely to find out.

In all fairness, she conceded, she shouldn't be angry with Kane for betraying her to Ned.

Kane wouldn't have viewed it as a betrayal.

At least Ned no longer saw her as a child whose hand needed to be held.

Ned had suggested she speak with Wellington.

Whereas Kane had advised that she should not.

Maybe she would throttle both of them.

Because of Harry's mysterious notebook, speaking to the Duke might well be akin to opening Pandora's box, and so Clea decided that for the moment she would not. She hadn't encountered the duke since her return to London, Wellington having more important matters to attend than social affairs.

Weak sunlight streamed through the library windows. From a desk drawer, Clea retrieved Ned's copy of the *Cryptography or the Art of Decyphering*. The little volume contained a series of rules and principles for creating and cracking codes and ciphers in a methodical way. Its leather cover was worn smooth by use.

Proposition One: the art of deciphering is the explanation of secret characters by certain rules. Proposition Two: Every language has, besides the form of characters, something peculiar in the place, order, continuation, frequency and number of the letters.

Clea flipped through the notebook. The unfamiliar handwriting was difficult to read. If no master code-breaker, she was sufficiently skilled to determine that, first, the coded entries weren't written in the simple Julius Caesar Cipher, in which a letter in the text was shifted a certain number of places down the alphabet; and, secondly, it *was* written in French. She drew a sheet of paper toward her and began to make notes.

A half hour and a headache later, Clea put down her pen and leaned back in her chair. Her efforts at deciphering having proved thus far unfruitful, she reached instead for Ovid's *Ibis*, an elegiac exercise in which the poet threatened an unknown enemy with a variety of gruesome fates, ranging from laming and blinding to cannibalism to death by pine cone.

Pine cone?

The object of the poet's curse was left unnamed.

The library was silent save for the crackling of the fire in the hearth and the scrabbling of mice in the walls.

It would be helpful, Clea thought, if she could determine the identity of her own enemy. Mariel Marsden might have been responsible for the man who had tried to snatch her outside Gunter's — had that incident been meant to truly harm or merely to terrify? — but Mariel had not been in the Chiado fruit market when Clea was accosted, nor at the inn with Pilar; hadn't traveled on shipboard with them. Moreover, the toplofty Mrs. Marsden was unlikely to consort with gentlemen of the road.

Or with the wretched little ragamuffin who had stolen Clea's Spanish pistol.

On the desk before her, alongside the *Ibis,* lay the double barrel folding trigger pistol given her by Kane. In case anyone attempted to 'interfere' with her in the library of Wakely Court.

Kane had refused to interfere with her. Because he was her brother's friend. Because she was one-and-twenty and he was almost twice as old.

Harry had been five-and-twenty when he died. Clea closed her eyes.

Memory served her up a *mélange* of images. Harry, sitting with Sabine Viccars and her husband Francis around the makeshift dinner table in that low-ceilinged Frenada farmhouse, exchanging the latest rumors, enjoying a bottle of Spanish wine, playing cards. Sabine and Harry dancing a minuet in a makeshift ballroom decorated to resemble a tent, draperies hiding the holes in the walls, a uniformed sentry guarding a great fissure in the ballroom floor.

Harry, collapsed on the banks of the Tagus River, his handsome face destroyed by a pistol shot to the head.

Francis Viccars died during the fall of Badajoz, on a moonlit night made brighter by immense French fireballs and exploding powder barrels and an endless barrage of shells. Badajoz had been one of the richest and most beautiful towns in the south of Spain, its siege one of the bloodiest in the Napoleonic Wars.

Sabine, too, was gone. Were there an afterlife, a concept about which she harbored doubts, Clea hoped Harry had met his friends there; that they were sitting together around some otherworldly table, enjoying a friendly game.

While she remained here, fending off ruffians and embracing — or attempting to embrace — rakehells.

The library door opened. Pilar entered the room, preceded by her pet. Fausto stalked toward the desk, leapt up and rearranged the various articles resting thereupon to his satisfaction, gave Clea a baleful glare. He next followed his tail three times in a circle, after which, his back turned pointedly toward her, he curled up for a snooze.

"Set aside your books, *querida!*" Pilar demanded. "We have a guest." Twinkling at the gentleman who had followed her into the library, the senhora arranged herself to good advantage on one of the carved chairs. Today she wore a splendidly fitted high-waisted, long-sleeved gown, its narrow skirt trimmed with rows of tucks above a worked flounce. Around her shoulders she had draped a beautifully embroidered, lavishly fringed triangular silk wrap. The entire ensemble was a brilliant pea-green.

Clea's unexpected guest was not reacting in the manner common to those first visiting her brother's library, which was generally slack-jawed amazement at the impenetrable muddle contained therein, though he did cast an appreciative glance at the eccentric chimneypiece. Clea slipped Harry's notebook and the *Cryptography* into the desk drawer. "Welcome to Wakely Court, Kit."

He strolled over to the desk, picked up the ugly statue. "A souvenir of your brother's war-time experiences, I presume?"

"I daresay you also brought back some souvenirs," Pilar observed brightly. "You must tell us what they were."

Idly, Clea stroked Fausto's back. The cat twitched an ear and stretched out to his full length.

One paw encountered the *Ibis*. Fausto opened one golden eye, contemplated the book, shoved it off the desk.

"*Ai!* Bad cat!" cried Pilar. "*Maroto!*" Fausto jumped down from the desk and darted through the open door. Pilar followed him, still scolding, out into the hall.

Kit picked up the fallen book. "That business in Berkeley Square— You had a close call. Has it occurred to you that you may be meddling in business someone would prefer you did not? I'd be no friend of Harry's if I didn't warn you to let sleeping dogs lie."

Kit would rather have been inspecting horseflesh at Tattersall's, Clea thought, ogling females in Hyde Park or placing some absurd wager in one of his clubs. She was reminded of Vienna, that great mummer's show. Kit had been attached to some official or another. She had waltzed with him the night before word of Napoleon's escape from Elba had turned the city on its ear.

"I have been tending to my own business for some time," she told him. "Not altogether successfully, granted, but that is beside the point. A person grows quite weary of people offering her advice."

"Point taken," Kit said dryly. He set the book back on the desk. "After our last conversation, I made some inquiries. Carruthers favors one particular gambling establishment. If you still wish to speak with him, I'll take you there tonight."

Chapter Nineteen

Sometimes even to live is an act of courage. — Seneca

The hour was growing late. Frankie longed for her bed. Not *her* bed, exactly, because she didn't have one, most often sleeping in night-cellar cubicles where the walls were smeared with grimy fingerprints and the ceilings scrawled with bawdy sketches, alongside slamkins and nibblers and fuddle-caps who poked elbows in her ribs and half-suffocated her with their breath.

Clea Marsden should have been snoozing in a proper bed with sweet-smelling sheets and no other bodies snoring in it at this very minute. But no, Lady Clea must wait till the household had quieted down and sneak out. She'd nearly snuck right past Frankie before Frankie realized what the ninny was about.

To say truth, which she didn't often, Frankie had no notion *what* Lady Clea was about. She'd been ready to give up her vigil and set out in search of a pint when her ladyship came creeping through the gardens toward a waiting rattler. Luckily, Frankie had been close enough to hear the direction Clea gave.

What business had a gentry mort in Bow Street at this time of night?

So well did Frankie know the byways of London that she reached Lady Clea's destination ahead of Clea herself. She ducked into the darkened doorway of a chandler's shop and settled down to wait, just another smelly slipgibbet in torn breeches and tattered jacket, patched shoes and a filthy felt hat.

Once, or so Frankie had been told, the nobs had lived in this neighborhood, prior to the Royal Opera House being built and the Bow Street Police Court taking up residence on the east side of the street. Shops, taverns and fancy houses had sat back a neat distance from the road. Today those same narrow structures were plastered with advertisements for every sort of patent medicine, alongside placards proclaiming plots to stake or boil or behead the Queen. Prostitutes and pickpockets prowled pavement littered with bits of fruit and vegetables left over from the Covent Garden market. A swell couldn't stroll about here even at midday without risking his handkerchief, pocket book or watch.

Frankie looked up at the theater, which had been built to resemble some Greek temple, and was decked out with fancy carvings and statues, all of which she considered a waste of good stone, save for the winged horse. As a child, Frankie had developed a fondness for that horse.

Old Ikey had trained her up to have a clever set of fambles. He'd sent her to pick pockets in company with other urchins, and always in an area with the largest crowds: the Strand, the Exchange, Covent Garden, Drury Lane. And then, business being business, he'd sold her to a female sharper who'd decided the presence of a brat would put the constables off her scent.

That had been a stroke of luck for Frankie. Earlene had been a dab hand herself. Among other things, she'd taught her new-bought bantling to talk half-proper, so as to expand their field of operations, flats tending to be suspicious, she said, of a female who spoke only flash. Frankie had waited in the shadows on those evenings Earlene rigged herself out in fancy togs and slipped into masquerades and other nobbish entertainments as easy as if she'd been to the manner born.

Women thieves regularly concealed stolen goods in large circular pockets worn under their skirts.

Earlene had wormed her way into the visitors' gallery in the Houses of Parliament. Churches attended by the nobs. Had even got into the general circle at St. James's Palace, where she'd been nabbed in possession of several gold trinkets, after which she'd paid her debt at Tyburn. When Earlene had died proud on the gallows, Frankie had been — she guessed — thirteen years of age.

She'd avoided Old Ikey after, not being wishful of dancing at the sheriff's ball herself.

Frankie squinted at the tavern opposite. She hoped Mr. Pritchett was off tracking down his counterfeiters instead of wetting his chaffer with a pint of ale whilst in pursuit of some pretty scoundrel or another. And speaking of doing what one shouldn't, here came Lady Clea, having put off her cloak and a fair amount of her other clothing, strutting down the street like a strumpet on the stroll. And who was that fellow with her, looking like he wished himself elsewhere?

They appeared to be having a difference of opinion. Lady Clea turned her back. The proper gent stood scowling as she marched up to the red baize door of a hell known as Mrs. Leach's due to the circumstance that punters frequently left the premises with their pockets cleaned out.

To Frankie's way of thinking, only a pig-widgeon wagered good coin on whether a certain card would be dealt from a wooden box, or a certain number turn up on a roll of the dice.

Good coin, or for that matter, bad.

Lady Clea had set to wheedling the porter, who stood barring her way, his arms crossed on his chest.

She handed him a folded piece of paper, followed by several coins. The porter pocketed the coins, shut the door in her face. Clea took up a position mere paces from the door, looking as if she meant to wait there until cockcrow. Her companion didn't join her, but stood nervously peering up and down the street.

A person might wonder how a gambling hell came to operate under the noses of the Bow Street beaks.

Because a beak could plump out his pockets with bribes from gamblers and whores, that's how.

A man-milliner in skin-tight calf-clingers staggered toward the doorway where Frankie was lounging, fumbling at his breeches as if he meant to take a piss.

A girl could withstand but so much temptation. Frankie stuck out her foot and caught her pigeon by the shoulders as he stumbled into her. The reek of cheap whiskey rocked her back on her heels.

"Hoi! Mind what you're at." Frankie briskly brushed him off, in the process ridding his pocket of its watch, and sent him on his way.

The drunken dandy staggered toward the gaming hell, leering at Lady Clea as he passed.

How long did Frankie have before he twigged that he'd lost his ticker? She stepped out of the doorway and into the street.

Clea wasn't paying heed to her surroundings. Her eyes were fixed on the red baize door. Frankie's own eye was caught by two rough-dressed bucks who stepped out of the nearby boozing-ken.

Frankie knew a blackguard when she saw one. These two made a fine example of wolves made up as sheep, one dark and one pale.

The dark man had a bandaged shoulder. The other was eyeing Lady Clea like a coney-catcher who'd spotted a fat hare.

Frankie looked about her. Clea's proper gent was nowhere to be seen.

A ginger-pated chap stepped out of the gaming hell. Clea called, "Carruthers!" He turned, saw her, froze.

The two blackguards moved forward. The dark man grabbed Clea's shoulders, spun her around. The other snatched the cove Clea had called Carruthers and slashed a blade across his throat.

Carruthers crumpled, blood gushing from his neck. Clea pulled a pistol from under her skirt and shot her assailant in the leg. He toppled over, howling and gripping his knee. Clea turned her pistol on the pale-haired man, pulled the trigger. It misfired. He grabbed her wrist, twisted the gun from her grasp.

Frankie hesitated. People who stuck their noses into other people's business were like to get them pinched right off. Still—

Screeching like a lovelorn tomcat, she ran forward and leapt onto the pale-haired man's back.

He twisted, cursing; flung her off him. Frankie howled as his blade sliced into her ribs. Clea swung round and punched her assailant in the nose.

Blood spurted. His hands flew to his face. He stepped back, tripped over the dark-haired knave still writhing on the ground, and fell on his arse. Clutching her side, Frankie kicked him in the twiddle-diddles, once and then again.

She staggered, fair mizzy-mazed from sight of her own claret spilling out so freely. Clea snatched up her little gun. The busybodies who'd crept closer to gawk scuttled back into the shadows. Pointing her pistol in their direction, Clea threw her other arm around Frankie, half-dragged and half-carried her around a corner, down an alley, and into a dark doorway where she let her slide to the ground.

Frankie yelped. Clea hitched up her skirts, tore off a strip of petticoat, and pressed it ungently against her ribs.

It hurt like bloody blazes.

Frankie fainted dead away.

Chapter Twenty

Circumstances rule men; men do not rule circumstances.
— Herodotus

His lantern held in front of him, Lord Saxe threaded his way through the cluttered attics of Wakely Court. Vague shapes lurked amid towering boxes and crates, peered around shrouded furniture and ominous artifacts, like phantasmal villains poised to strike. Giles Lawrence followed close on his heels.

" 'By the pricking of my thumbs'," Giles murmured, when behind them ancient floorboards creaked as if from the weight of unseen feet. "In surroundings such as this, one can almost believe in ghosts."

Kane wasn't sure, sometimes, that he *didn't* believe in ghosts. In this case, however, the source of the mysterious noises was probably nothing more otherworldly than the senhora's cat.

" 'Something wicked this way comes'," Giles added, as the floorboards creaked again.

Mr. Bloody Lawrence was enjoying himself far too much. Kane approached a far, dark corner where all manner of wicked somethings might gather to whisper and plot. The Jacobean sideboard that usually stood beneath a moth-eaten tapestry had been pushed aside, revealing a small doorway that opened onto a passage built into the thickness of the wall.

Candlelight, and Pilar's voice, drifted down the stairwell. "*Fazei-vos mel, comer-vox-ão as moscas.* He that makes himself an ass must not take it ill if men ride him."

She sounded cross.

Silently cursing the circumstance that Giles had been drinking port with him when he received Pilar's summons, and his own stupidity in not keeping the nature of that summons to himself, Kane mounted the steep stair.

At the top, a second door stood open. Beyond it lay Clea's secret retreat. The servants weren't supposed to know of the turret room's existence, though Tidcombe must surely suspect.

Pilar had not stopped scolding. She paused, arms akimbo, as the men entered the room.

" 'How now, you secret, black, and midnight hags!' " quoth Giles. "No offense intended, Senhora Estevez. We have come from a production of *Macbeth* at Covent Garden, and I remain under the influence of the Bard."

"You are obviously under the influence of something," Pilar observed tartly. "But better late than never, no?"

Several lighted candles had been set around the chamber, illuminating the faded Chinese wall-paper, the Oriental rugs that cushioned the wooden floor. Ancient window curtains had been drawn against the night.

In one shadowy corner, a long daybed was piled high with faded pillows. On a table drawn up beside it rested a basin filled with bloody water, and a pile of soiled rags.

Kane stared at the slight figure that lay beneath the tasseled coverlet. Pilar's note had requested that he present himself at once. It hadn't explained why.

"Why are you here?" a familiar voice demanded. Kane swung round to find Clea sitting, scowling, in a chair carved with roses and daisies and strawberry blossoms, a caterpillar worked cunningly into the design.

She wasn't injured. As his heart descended from his throat back down where it belonged, Kane first felt relieved, and then even more cross.

"Why do you think he's here?" inquired Pilar. "I sent for him, of course."

Giles drifted toward the chimney wall, from which vantage point a painted gentleman contemplated his surroundings with faintly amused ennui. " 'Your face, my thane, is as a book where men may read strange matters'," he quoted. "Not to belabor a theme."

It was Kane who felt belabored. Or beleaguered. Too late, unfortunately, to shove his unwanted companion down the stairs.

Clea also glanced at the portrait. "That is Francis Wakely, and he was a Restoration rake. This is, or was, his house." She gestured to the swath of fabric she had draped around her shoulders. "And this is his cloak."

Antique black velvet. Tarnished gold lace. Pearl embroidery. Kane said, impatiently, "I doubt Pilar summoned me here to admire your costume." Then he took a closer look at what Clea was wearing — or not wearing — under Francis Wakely's cloak and briefly lost his powers of speech.

Now that she'd grown breasts, Clea seemed determined to display them to the world.

Both Pilar and Clea were disheveled, he realized belatedly, with water-spotted clothing and disarranged hair. While Clea had made herself up like a strumpet, Pilar was unusually subdued in a demure dress of printed muslin, white strewn with lilac flowers, its full sleeves edged with lace at the wrists and scalloped flounces at the hemline.

The gown's demure effect was offset by the fact the senhora had left off her stays.

She stamped a dainty foot. "Will you tell him, *querida,* or must I?"

Giles turned away from the portrait. "Ah, explanations. Do proceed."

"*Obrigado!*" Pilar snapped. "Clea has had another mishap. Which is the eighth, at last count. Although I doubt it can fairly be called a mishap when someone sticks a knife into a person's throat."

With a massive effort of will, Kane elevated his attention from Clea's bosom to her neck.

"Not *my* throat. Clive Carruthers is dead." Tersely, Clea explained. "Luckily, the coach was waiting where we left it. I don't know what became of Kit."

The turret room was warm, its chimney wall providing more than adequate heat. Nevertheless, Kane experienced a chill. "Carruthers!" he snarled. "Ned—"

"You and Ned between you were hardly helpful," Clea interrupted. "Surely you didn't expect I would sit quietly at home twiddling my thumbs."

Twiddle. To toy with idly, especially with the fingers. Kane's chill was swallowed by a wave of heat that had nothing to do with any chimney walls. "You say you shot one assailant and bloodied the other's nose. If it was my pistol you were carrying, you had a shot left."

"Contrary to rumor, I am not by nature murderously inclined," Clea retorted. "In any event, your pistol misfired."

Giles had been, during this conversation, wandering around the small room, inspecting in turn a deck of Italian playing cards, an ivory rosary with a pendant death mask, an ornate sweetmeat box. " 'Fair is foul, and foul is fair'," he offered as he sat down gingerly on the edge of the day bed, thereby rousing the senhora's cat, which had curled up amid the pillows for a snooze.

The blasted feline couldn't have been responsible for the attic's creaking floorboards, Kane realized.

He surveyed the daybed, and the small motionless figure burrowed so deep into the bedding that he could only see a slice of pale cheek and a mop of dark blonde hair. "This is the brat?"

"My little filcher," agreed Clea. "Or my guardian angel. She refuses to waken so I can ask her which she is. I would also like to ask if she was following me, or just happened to be in the wrong place at the wrong time. Or the right time, for my sake."

"She?"

"Oho! 'Is this a dagger that I see before me?' " inquired Giles.

"*Santo Deus!*" snapped Pilar. "Can you not be serious for one little moment? Here we are, in possession of a young person who is not as young as one might think and furthermore goes about in the guise of an odiferous boy." She wrinkled her nose. "I think we should have her rags destroyed. She can hardly escape — if she is so foolish as to wish to escape when instead she can stay here and be properly fed, which she clearly has not been for some time — without any clothes."

Clea remarked, "Julie did."

Giles looked intrigued. "Julie being your brother's wife?"

Clea ignored his question. "We brought our guest in through the tunnels. No one knows she's here. I'm not convinced we shouldn't call in a doctor, Pilar."

"You are as skilled a nurse as any English *médico*," the senhora protested. "Her wound is not so dangerous, though it will prevent her picking pockets for a while."

"Tunnels?" Giles echoed.

Clea glanced at him. "This old house has many secrets. A passage in my dressing room leads out into the garden through the old Tudor drains."

Kane scowled. Clea had just told Giles how to steal into her bedchamber.

Definitely, he should have shoved the bastard down the stairs.

Clea had retrieved the folding pistol, unreliable as it might be, and was holding it casually aimed at the daybed. "Are you planning to shoot the brat?" Kane asked.

"It would be highly ungrateful, seeing as she risked her neck for mine." Clea met his gaze. "I suspect Clive was killed to prevent him talking to me, but why? I was disguised."

"Your disguise," Kane informed her bluntly, "isn't half as clever as you imagine. Once a man gets over being distracted by your bosom, your face is easily recognizable beneath its paint."

" 'My mistress's eyes are like the sun'," quoth Giles. " 'If snow be white, why then her breasts are dun'."

"Must you?" Pilar demanded. "We have more serious matters to consider than Clea's bosom, senhor."

Clea drew her cloak more tightly around her, thereby removing said bosom from public view. "One of those men had a bandaged shoulder. He might have been my highwayman, in which case I have now shot him twice. And again, he might not have been. Maybe this has nothing to do with me. Not even Pilar knew I was going to Bow Street."

Not trusting himself to make a civil comment, Kane walked closer to the daybed. The brat hadn't stirred since he first glimpsed her. He reached out and brushed back her hair to reveal her face.

It was a surprisingly pretty face. Kane doubted it had ever before been this clean. "I wouldn't open my eyes either in your place,

Frankie," he told her, his tone grim.

"Frankie?" Pilar inquired.

The brat's eyelids quivered. Kane said, "She's one of Pritchett's strays."

"Pritchett?" echoed Clea. "The Bow Street Runner? I don't understand."

Nor did Kane, but he intended to. He grasped one freshly scrubbed earlobe, and pinched.

Frankie did open her eyes, then. She squinted at the people gathered around the daybed, and squeezed them shut again.

"Least said, soonest mended," murmured Giles. "Wise child."

Chapter Twenty-One

Meet the misfortune as it comes. — Perseus

The Academy was quiet. Heavy draperies muffled the noises of the street outside. Clea wondered how much longer Mrs. Kingston meant to keep her waiting. At this rate, she would soon wear a path in the sitting room's exquisitely woven rug.

She studied the large oil painting that hung above the fireplace, Lilah herself, gloriously nude, hair unbound and streaming down her back; and then a set of exceptionally fine reproductions of William Hogarth's *A Harlot's Progress* on an opposite wall. According to rumor, Mrs. Kingston had once eaten a thousand-guinea banknote on a slice of bread to prove she could afford to be selective about whom she took to her bed.

Clea resumed her pacing. Were she sensible, she would hurry back to Wakely Court and leave someone else to clear up this mess. But it was *her* mess, wasn't it, and it had started with Harry's death, and consequently here she stood, in a Paphian's parlor, waiting for an audience.

She picked up a porcelain figurine, recognized its erotic nature, set the Harlequin back in its place and continued her inspection of the room.

Hopefully, Pilar would not realize she had slipped away again and raise the alarm.

Clea had left her friend in the turret room, shuffling the old deck of Italian playing cards, showing Frankie how to cheat. Fausto, who had developed an unfathomable fondness for their guest, had been snoozing in his usual spot on the daybed.

Frankie couldn't be kept hidden away in the turret room forever. What was to be done with her, once this business was resolved?

Were the girl to continue on her present path, she'd sooner or later thrust her neck into a noose.

Clea touched a finger to the cool surface of a Chinese porcelain jar. The exterior portrayed a woman in a study, the interior that same woman in a considerably more intimate scene.

Whatever Carruthers had felt on seeing her waiting in the street outside the gaming hell — dismay? displeasure? — his expression had shifted to shock as the sharp blade sliced across his throat.

And what on earth had happened to Kit Graham?

The sitting room door opened. Lilah Kingston entered, followed by a handsome footman carrying a tall chocolate pot on a silver tray. She was the picture of propriety in her long-sleeved high-necked muslin morning gown, her heavy chestnut hair drawn back in a prim coil.

The footman placed his tray on a table and backed away, closing the door behind him. Mrs. Kingston regarded her guest. "I apologize for keeping you waiting, Lady Clea. I have not yet had my morning chocolate. You will join me, I hope."

Clea threw back her veil. "I congratulate you, Mrs. Kingston. Your servants are remarkably well-trained. Not one so much as blinked at the arrival of a strange female on your doorstep."

"It would take a great deal to surprise my staff, given the nature of this house." Mrs. Kingston applied a whisk to the contents of the chocolate pot.

Clea contemplated the incongruity of a brothel owner engaged in so domestic an activity as the preparation of hot chocolate. Then she contemplated the other activities in which her hostess might find herself engaged, and with whom, and was tempted to empty the chocolate pot over her head.

Mrs. Kingston looked amused, as if she had some inkling of her caller's inclinations. "Pray be seated, Lady Clea. You have come to speak with me about the late Viscount Carruthers, I presume."

Clea sank down on the satin-upholstered loveseat. "You don't seem overly disturbed by his death."

Mrs. Kingston poured the chocolate into tall, narrow cups. "You cannot be so naïve as to assume I cherish tender feelings for every man who has shared my bed."

Clea was not so naïve as to be lured into a discussion of Mrs. Kingston's bedmates. "You might like to know that the viscount's throat was cut. I saw it done myself."

Mrs. Kingston raised her eyebrows. " 'Might like to know'? What an odd idea you have of me. As a point of curiosity, how did you come to be present when the viscount, ah, marched off this mortal coil?"

"I didn't mean that you would enjoy the fact, but being informed of it. Being as the manner of his demise was not mentioned in the newssheets." Clea paused as Mrs. Kingston handed her a cup. "As for how I happened to be present, a friend told me where Carruthers might be found."

Mrs. Kingston regarded Clea over the brim of her own cup. "You are either very foolish, my lady, or very bold."

"Since I am sitting in your parlor, we may assume that I am both." Clea tasted her chocolate, which was strong and spicy, with hints of nutmeg and cinnamon. "Clive was a friend of my husband's. I had hoped to speak with him. And speaking of speaking, a woman in your position must hear many things."

"A woman engaged in my profession, you mean, gentlemen under the influence of liquor, or lust, tending to be indiscrete? In the non-Biblical sense, I did not know Carruthers well. Even if I had, he was not the sort of man to spill his secrets to a whore. Though he was wont to spill his substance easily enough." Mrs. Kingston smiled.

Clea conceded defeat. If Lilah Kingston guessed a client's secrets, she would keep her conclusions to herself.

Discretion, Clea supposed, was a virtue in a female of Mrs. Kingston's 'profession'.

And why should the woman confide in a stranger, after all?

Would Mrs. Kingston confide in Kane? Would he repeat those confidences, if she did?

Once, Clea had waited for Kane to notice that she had finished growing up; had planned, after she was equipped with bosoms, to place herself naked in his bed. Now she thought that bed would be very crowded, with Lilah Kingston — and how many others? — already ensconced there.

She set down her chocolate cup. "I must return to Wakely Court before I'm missed."

"I have enjoyed our conversation. Seldom am I privileged to discuss anything beyond prophylactics and aphrodisiacs." Mrs. Kingston rose, approached a mahogany writing desk, pulled open a drawer. "Permit me to make you a gift. This is a concoction of various ingredients meant to strengthen the heart and quicken the senses, allay nervous irritability and provide stimulus to the brain; and also to make the body invincible against the venom of serpents, spiders and toads."

Clea eyed it skeptically. "I doubt I'm going to be bit by a toad."

"No, but you may be stung by a serpent. I had intended Kane to give this to you, but since you're here—" Mrs. Kingston held out a small vial.

Startled by the woman's insistence, Clea took the little glass container from her hand.

Mrs. Kingston closed the drawer. "Among my various enterprises is a Temple of Beauty. I could provide you with Favorite of the Harem's Pearl White Powder for the skin, or Indian Coal for enhancing the eyes. Not that you have need of such concoctions. Yet."

Clea felt like one of Pilar's mouses, being toyed with by a sleek, sophisticated, lavender-eyed cat. She murmured, "You are too kind."

"Sarcasm," remarked Mrs. Kingston, "is the language of the devil. If I may go on? *You* may like to know that Mariel Marsden visited the Temple in search of something, she claimed, to help her sleep. A stronger potion than can be purchased from a pharmacist. In other words, a potential poison. I have just handed you the antidote."

Clea's fingers tightened around the little vial. She had almost forgotten Mariel in the midst of other recent events.

Mrs. Kingston added, "London is a dangerous city. I suggest you pay particular attention to what you eat and drink."

Clea glanced at her chocolate cup.

Mrs. Kingston said, drily, "I assure you, Lady Clea—"

Before she could finish her sentence, the parlor door flew open with such force that it crashed against the wall.

Chapter Twenty-Two

Dishonor will not trouble me, once I am dead. —
Euripides

"I assure you, Lady Clea—" Lilah broke off as Kane strode into the room.

Clea turned a startled face toward him. Lilah said, ironically, "Heigh ho! We are undone."

She found the situation amusing? Kane experienced a strong urge to slap the smile off Lilah's face.

He turned his wrath on Clea. "What in *Hades* were you thinking? Or are your brains grown so addled that you have ceased considering consequences before you act?"

Her brows snapped together. "If we are to engage in plain-speaking, *you* are a sneaksby, a bully, and a babblemouth to boot."

He must not manhandle her, Kane warned himself. And he most definitely must not toss her onto the loveseat, yank up her skirts and bury himself in her sweet heat.

Lilah moved toward the door. Behind her, the latch snicked shut.

Clea crossed her arms beneath her bosom. "First Frankie was dogging my footsteps, and now you've set your spies on me. Soon I'll be leading a full-blown parade around the town."

"Not if you are locked in the turret room with Frankie," Kane retorted grimly.

She narrowed her eyes at him. "Never assume I couldn't escape."

Kane didn't doubt her, Wakely Court being what it was. Maybe he should have Clea locked up in the Tower instead.

She would probably escape that also. Clea would remain nowhere she didn't want to be. He said, "If you had a grain of the sense God gave a goose—"

Clea interrupted, "Draw in your horns! I wasn't wandering the streets without an escort."

"I daresay you left your footman at a coffee house," Kane snarled. "Not caring to corrupt his morals. Leaving yourself without any protection whatsoever in the meantime."

Clea bit her lip.

She didn't *look* like a madwoman, Kane admitted, in that ugly bonnet, serviceable dark gown and shawl. She might have been a maidservant, arranging to put her leisure hours to profitable use.

It was his wits that had gone wandering. Else he would not be so vividly recalling how he'd admired her in a harlot's clothes. "Wholly aside from the fact that you are behaving like the hen-brained heroine of some horrid novel there is the matter of your reputation, which would be in tatters were it to become public knowledge that you visited the Academy. Bad enough that you were seen speaking with Lilah in Hyde Park, but *this*—"

"Hang my reputation!" snapped Clea. "You truly have become a prude. Ned's footman has no notion where I went from the coffee house, and Mrs. Kingston's servants don't know who I am. For my presence in this house to become public knowledge, either you or Mrs. Kingston would have to betray me to the press."

Kane didn't comment. Clea had taken off her shawl and he was briefly distracted by a desire to see her further disrobe.

She sat down on the loveseat. "I know what I'm doing, Kane."

"Indeed. And what is that?"

"*Not* to quiz your inamorata about you, if that's what you're thinking." Kane flinched, and Clea sighed. "Forget I said that. I had hoped Mrs. Kingston might have information that would help me in my inquiries, but she says she doesn't. It may even be true."

Kane was not, in that moment, concerned with what Lilah might or might not know. "Clea—"

She shook her head. "It's true I sometimes fail to foresee the consequences of my actions, such as when I took Frankie to Wakely

Court. That seemed a good idea in the moment, but afterward I thought, what better way for a pilferer to worm her way into the house? The girl probably plans to abscond with Ned's silver plate."

Kane frowned. If Clea was trying to distract him, she'd succeeded. Had Frankie been in on this business from the first? He retrieved the brandy decanter from its accustomed resting place, despite the earliness of the hour.

Clea cleared her throat. Remembering the last time they had drunk brandy together, Kane poured liquor into a second glass, handed it to her.

She took the snifter from him. Her fingers brushed his. While his back was turned, Kane realized, she'd removed her gloves.

A frisson of anticipation shimmered down his spine.

Clea sipped her brandy, swallowed, shivered slightly. "Frankie is close-mouthed as an oyster. When pressed for information, she informed us that she had already put in her oar and as a result been left in the lurch, and was therefore pitch-kettled as to why anyone should judge her such a chucklehead as to jaw on about the thatch-gallows who'd tried to gut her like a fish. However, she agrees her presence is best kept secret from the servants and thus far has refrained from attempting to explore the rest of the house. When her curiosity overcomes her scruples, as invariably it will, Frankie will discover she is locked away as securely as in any gaol."

"Street urchins seldom have the luxury of scruples," Kane pointed out. Difficult to say if an enemy imprisoned in the attics of Wakely Court was better than an enemy left free to roam the streets, or worse.

Regarding him thoughtfully through her lowered lashes, Clea licked brandy off her lower lip.

Clearly, the woman meant to drive him mad.

Kane had gone to great effort to keep the more titillating details of Viscount Carruthers's demise out of the newspapers, which were too busy relating Caroline's antics to waste much print on the death of yet another drunken peer. Consequently, the Polite World remained unaware that Lady Clea Marsden had been wandering the streets dressed like a tart when the viscount got his throat slit.

Yet, despite all his efforts to protect her, here she sat in a whore's parlor, looking simultaneously provocative and innocent. A better man than he would be determining how to protect her from himself. Kane drank deeply from his glass.

Clea set her snifter aside. "For each step I take forward, and there have been precious few of them, I slip back several more. I feel as if I am attempting to push a massive boulder up a very steep hill. Harry would know what all this is about. Perhaps I should hold a séance."

Kane very much disliked this notion. "Ferreting out who killed your husband won't bring him back to life."

"I've no desire to arrange a resurrection. Retribution, however, is a very different thing." From her reticule, Clea removed a little vial. "Mrs. Kingston gave this to me. It is an antidote, she claims, to a powerful sleeping draught that Mariel Marsden purchased in her shop."

Kane reminded himself to speak with Lilah about the sale of soporifics.

And with Amory Marsden about his mother's malice. Maybe they should lock *her* in the turret room.

Clea replaced the vial in her reticule. "I've no desire to join Harry. Wherever he may be. And now, if you don't mind, I would prefer not to talk about him any more."

She rose and walked purposefully toward him. Kane put down his glass.

A better man would back away.

His feet, alas, refused to function.

He had poured her brandy, after all.

And hoped that she might drink it.

Opportunist that he was.

She halted less than a hair's breadth away. Kane inhaled her sweet perfume. "I'm *not* a prude," he said.

She slid her arms around his neck. "Prove it. If you dare."

If he dared? Even as Kane reminded himself that he possessed scruples, dilatory though they might be, he was at the same time caressing her cheek, her chin, the tip of her nose. His mouth trailed along her throat, lingered against the pulse beating wildly there.

She threaded her fingers in his hair. "Kiss me properly, damn you," she demanded.

Kane drew her even closer, claiming her sweet brandy-flavored mouth.

Or maybe she claimed him.

Many moments later, when they were forced to pause for breath, Kane found himself sitting on the loveseat with Clea on his lap. Her bonnet perched tipsily atop the antique porcelain jar. The fastenings of her gown were half-undone. This was, he decided fuzzily, a perfect example of why a lady should never be left with a gentleman unchaperoned.

Not that there was much of the gentleman about him at the moment.

And Clea's behavior could hardly be called ladylike.

She had taken him by surprise, or surely Kane wouldn't have—

Claptrap. Of course he would.

Clea rested her curly head against his shoulder. "I shouldn't have done that."

"Nor should I," he agreed.

"But since we did—" Clea lifted one hand to touch his cheek. His fingers brushed against her breasts, lingered there.

"Ah," said Lilah from the doorway. "You have resolved your differences, I see."

Kane snatched his hand away.

Chapter Twenty-Three

Fishes live in the sea, as men do on land: the great ones
eat up the little ones. — Pericles

In Threadneedle Street, behind the Royal Exchange and westward, the Bank of England squatted like a hen atop an egg-filled nest.

A balustrade and handsome vases adorned the top of the stone building. On the face of the pediment Britannia sat with shield and spear, at her feet a cornucopia pouring out fruit. A grand gate opened into a courtyard and beyond it a great hall of the Corinthian order, a statue of King William III in a niche at the upper end. Behind the courtyard lay another quadrangle, an arcade on the east and west sides, and an accountant's office on the north. Over this and the other end of the quadrangle were handsome apartments, and a fine fretworked staircase. Under it were large vaults, with strong walls and iron gates.

In one of those vaults, Mr. Pritchett of Bow Street stood watching the contents of a money-bag being counted and examined, result of one of the tellers having been seen sorting, in a suspicious manner, new guineas from old. Pritchett was not in a pleasant mood, having earlier that day been hit over the head with an iron saucepan whilst apprehending an enterprising group of coiners headquartered in Kent Street. For his part in the arrest, he would receive a mere ten pounds.

"Short." The bank official, a rotund individual with a sparse few strands of hair combed across his shiny skull, held a guinea close to his lamp and examined the coin's edge. "And this has recently been filed."

He dropped the guinea on a jeweler's scale. No one in the room was surprised when the coin weighed light.

"The directors won't be happy." The official pulled a handkerchief from his pocket and wiped his brow.

"There'll soon be one less coiner to contend with," Pritchett told him. "Your directors will like that. And it was your sharp eye as caught out the miscreant, which I will be happy to point out."

The official brightened. "So it was."

So it hadn't been, as they both knew full well. The sharp-eyed clerk who'd peached on his fellow worker would gain his own reward.

Pritchett departed, not by the bank's main entrance but the back. No directors sat in the parlor; the clerks and tellers, engravers and bank-note printers had gone home. The transfer-office was dark. He crossed the courtyard, empty now of the coaches and wagons that frequently arrived loaded with gold and silver; passed through the gate into Bartholomew Lane, where he collected the constable he'd left waiting there.

Bartholomew Lane to Threadneedle to Broad Street: the evening was damp and the streets less busy than was common, most people being engaged with their suppers at this hour. Pritchett wondered if they'd find the ambitious Mr. Wiggins — described by his irate employer as 'death's head on a mopstick with straw-colored hair' — enjoying a last meal of pickled whelks and hot eels.

Pritchett wished him joy of it. When a man couldn't trust a banker, who *could* he trust?

Once, Broad Street had been one of the widest streets within the medieval city walls. Pritchett paused in front of a plain brick building, three storeys and an attic with a tiled roof. The entrance doorway of Number Eight boasted a flat projecting hood supported on carved wood brackets. Pritchett applied the gilt head of his baton to the door.

The person who responded to his summons — shirt sleeves rolled up, a napkin tucked into the collar of his shirt — was cadaverous, with a shock of yellow hair. Pritchett said, "Frederick Wiggin, I presume?"

The man looked nervous. "Who wants to know?"

"Bow Street. In other words, my lad, your cat has got out of its bag."

Wiggins protested, predictably, that he was innocent as a babe newborn. Ignoring this nonsense, Pritchett pushed past him and into the apartment. A quick inspection revealed rooms for eating, living, sleeping — and a locked door.

Pritchett took a set of picklocks from inside his coat: Betty, Jenny, Kate. Ruminating on the circumstance of lock picks being called after females, he had the door open in a trice.

Beyond it lay what might in a grander establishment have served as a dressing room. Pritchett's eye was immediately drawn to a mahogany secretaire with several graduated drawers and a fall-front that hid more drawers, pigeon holes, and a writing surface.

Rather, a working surface. In the secondary drawers, he uncovered vise, files, two bags of gold filings and a clever machine designed to remill gold guineas that had been filed down.

He also discovered a hundred gold guineas, pristine, not yet filed.

Pritchett returned to the main room, carrying vise, files, and gold filings. Wiggins tried unsuccessfully to twist out of the constable's firm grasp. "What's that you have there? I never saw those things before."

Pritchett tsk'd. "Next you'll try and tell me you've not been diddling your employer. You may spare your breath."

Wiggins licked dry lips. "I don't know what you expect I've done, but I swear I didn't. You're making a mistake."

Pritchett hefted his baton, slammed its gilt head hard into Wiggin's ribs. "What you are is a queer cole maker in the employment of the Bank of England, whose trust you have so betrayed as to abstract guineas from your drawer, carrying them home and later returning the altered coins to the Bank. In case you didn't know it, the trustees take unkindly to activities of that sort."

Wiggins straightened, gasping for air.

Pritchett gestured to the constable. "Wait outside."

The constable had assisted Pritchett on other such occasions and therefore knew that any irregularities, if unremarked, would be amply rewarded. He withdrew, quietly closing the door.

Pritchett pulled out his pistol, not taking any chances on his person being further abused. Wiggins goggled wide-eyed at him, like a rabbit caught by a snake's stare.

"You and me are going to trade confidences," explained Pritchett. "So to speak. It's my duty to remind you that coining and counterfeiting are classified as High Treason, result of coins bearing the image of the King. Not so many years past, men caught engaging in the practice were drawn and quartered. Women were strangled and burnt at the stake. These days, few judged guilty of forgery can hope to escape being hanged."

As if his legs grew weak, Wiggins clutched the back of a chair.

"It's all up with you, cully," Pritchett continued. "You're well and truly nabbed. However, if I was to put in a word, it might be possible for you to be transported instead of shaking Jack Ketch's hand." He paused. "*If* I was to put in a word."

Moments later, the constable departed with the teller in his charge. Pritchett departed also, the richer by a hundred gold guineas, pristine. He deposited his ill-gotten gains in a hidey-hole known solely to himself, then retired to a nearby oyster cellar to reward his labors with a pint.

The cellar was small and warm and dark, and stank of tallow candles. Customers crowded around wooden tables crammed into an L-shaped room. Pritchett waved aside oysters and rizzared haddock and settled down with his ale.

Conversations swirled around him, most of which had to do with the proceedings currently underway in the House. One of the defense witnesses had provided the clearest testimony thus far that the prosecution witnesses had been bribed, thereby opening the case for the Crown to charges of false evidence, subornation of perjury and, in the case of the Commissioners, a criminal lack of control over their agents. As result, the House was divided, the Whig Lords weighing in behind the Queen.

Pritchett had little interest in the business. In his opinion, a queen shouldn't go about acting like a tart. For that matter, neither should a king.

And viscounts shouldn't meddle in matters that didn't concern them and consequently get theirs throat slit.

Nor should little whores. Red Mary had been found underneath a cart in Covent Garden with her throat gaping open like a second mouth.

A dead whore who resembled Clea Fairchild led Pritchett's

thoughts down pathways he was reluctant to tread.

"There you are," said a familiar voice. A chill crept down Pritchett's spine.

He peered into the shadows. A familiar figure was seated in an adjacent chair. Mere moments past that chair had been occupied by a workman whose clothing stank of horses, an aroma Pritchett far preferred to the scented soap that put him in mind of brimstone.

Boiling blood and burning sand.

Being fed upon by harpies.

Torn apart by rabid dogs.

Prior to his acquaintance with the Deacon, Pritchett had not realized his mind was of such a melodramatic bent.

A serving girl approached the table, cast the Deacon a flirtatious glance. The look he gave her in return caused her to back hastily away.

The Deacon flicked open his snuffbox. "When were you going to inform me that the Marsdens hired Bow Street to find out the facts of Harry Marsden's death, specifically if his wife had been involved?"

Pritchett didn't dare ask what lay behind the Deacon's interest in the Marsdens. "I thought you already knew."

"I do not," the Deacon said softly, "require you to think. Rumor has it that if Clea Marsden — or one of her many lovers — didn't actually pull the trigger, her numerous betrayals caused her husband to shoot himself."

Lady Clea a lightskirt? Pritchett blinked.

"I *do* require that rumor reaches the proper ears," the Deacon added. "I trust you understand."

Pritchett understood that where knowledge could get a man's throat slit, ignorance was bliss. He beckoned a serving girl to bring him another pint.

Chapter Twenty-Four

Second thoughts are ever wiser. — Euripides

Clea was deep in a fit of the blue devils. She greatly regretted her misbehavior with Kane.

She'd acted like a harlot. No wonder he had pulled her down on his lap and ravished her with his mouth.

How many times had Kane sat on that same loveseat with his mistress on his lap?

His kisses meant little, she reminded herself. Kane must have kissed a thousand women to learn to kiss to such good effect.

She glanced around the library. Her gaze lingered on the bookshelves, which hid a sliding panel and a hidden staircase.

Once she had knelt on the floor in front of these same bookshelves, playing marbles with Ned and Kane.

Even then, she'd wanted to misbehave with Kane.

Clea moved the library steps into position; climbed to inspect a dusty shelf. *Inglish Orthoggraphy Epittomized*; *Rudiments of English Grammar*; *Philosophy of Rhetoric*—

She plucked a battered lexicon from amongst the other volumes and descended the steps, thinking now not of Kane but of Frenada, remembering Major Scoville seated at his table surrounded by captured scraps of paper brought in by the guerrillas, drawing up tables marked in columns of numbers, fashioning his code-cracking charts.

Currently, Scoville was serving as colonel in command of the Royal Wagon Train, in which position he passed his time watching drivers and wagons travel round and round the square at Croyden. The major hadn't numbered among the loyal staff members whom Wellington had advanced to the new battlefield of the House of Commons, Scoville's reform-mindedness and lowly social standing rendering him unsuitable as a Tory MP.

Wellington. Clea sympathized with Hamlet. Whether to take arms against a sea of troubles...

Or, as Pilar would have it, *Deus ajuda os que se ajudam.* Heaven helps those who help themselves.

Meanwhile, on a barren rock in the midst of a vast ocean, the one-time Emperor of the French bathed in a stone garden reservoir, result of his bathroom floor having rotted in the damp climate and collapsed.

Clea seated herself at Ned's desk, Kane's folding pistol within easy reach, and opened the lexicon. From its hollowed-out interior, she removed the battered notebook she'd taken from Harry's trunk. Next she opened the desk drawer, withdrew the *Cyptography.*

Conradus provided much advice about deciphering French: 'e' was the most commonly used letter; words ending in double letters likely ended in 'ee'; 'et' was the most oft repeated word. A single letter on its own was an ' a', 'y', or a constant with an apostrophe.

Some of the notebook entries seemed to be straightforward descriptions of battles witnessed, appointments made and kept; but others— Clea squinted at a series of scrawled numbers. Could it be a date? Co-ordinates of some sort?

"Harry," she said aloud. "What on earth *is* this?"

Clea started half out of her skin when she heard a scratching at the door. She had hardly expected a reply.

The door opened. "Mister Lawrence assures me you will wish to speak with him, my lady," Tidcombe announced.

"And so I do, Thank you, Tidcombe." The butler departed, dripping disapproval. Clea shoved the *Cryptography* and Harry's notebook into the desk drawer.

Moments later, Giles strolled into the room. "Lady Clea. I am fortunate to catch you alone. How does your houseguest?"

Clea folded her hands atop the empty lexicon. "Frankie is sulking because we won't permit her to have a weapon. I am frequently forced to remind myself that she is here result of having gotten a knife in the ribs after rushing to my defense. *Why* she rushed to help me, I haven't yet determined. If an altruistic impulse tapped that one on the shoulder, she'd darken its daylights."

Giles studied her face. "Would you have shot your assailant, had Kane's gun not misfired?"

"Bloodthirsty wench that I am? Since the gun *did* misfire, we will never know. Frankie is of the opinion that I should have blown out the bugger's brains. Her words, not mine."

He smiled. "It's a bloody-minded brat. Are you aware of the Chinese proverb that says if you save someone's life, you become responsible for them?"

Clea shuddered. "Fortunately, I am not Chinese. Have you learned anything more about Kit Graham, Giles?"

His amusement faded. "I have not. The man seems to have left London. His lodgings have been cleaned out."

By Kit himself? Or someone else? Clea said aloud, "Maybe Lilah Kingston has heard some news of Kit."

"I beg you, say no more," Giles pleaded. "If you do not take me into your confidence, Kane will have no good reason to challenge me to pistols at dawn. I wouldn't want to have to shoot him, you see."

Clea eyed him, distracted. "You're certain that you're the better shot?"

"Can you be certain I am not?" Giles studied her face. "Much as I dislike to give advice, I feel compelled to in this instance, being as you seem determined to become bosom-bows with the frail but fair. To wit: do bear in mind that Lilah Kingston is a female with her eye to the main chance."

Giles knew that she had visited King's Place? How? "Interesting that you should call Mrs. Kingston an opportunist," Clea remarked. "I've heard the same said of you."

Giles picked up the hippopotamus-headed statue. " 'Be thou as chaste as ice, as pure as snow, thou shall not escape calumny.' As you are experiencing first-hand."

Giles Lawrence knew how it felt to be a favorite of the gossips. Clea leaned back in her chair. "That figure you are caressing is Taweret, Egyptian goddess of fertility and childbirth."

"The female hippopotamus is a fearsome creature. Somewhat like yourself." He returned the statue to its place on the desk. "Had you summoned a constable when you were accosted in Bow Street, you might have discovered your villain's identity and thereby spared yourself subsequent mishaps."

"If I had summoned a constable to Bow Street," Clea pointed out, "the whole world would have discovered who *I* was. Contrary to popular opinion, I am not a feather-head."

"To whose opinion do you refer? Shall I venture a guess?"

"I would prefer you did not. What's your stake in all this, Giles? Don't bother telling me you don't have one. Did Kane engage you to ferret out the details of Harry's death?"

He shrugged. "You make me sound so mercenary. Kane didn't 'engage' me, precisely. I offered to help."

Giles Lawrence, in Clea's experience, was most inclined to help himself. "I didn't realize you are so altruistic. Very well, what *have* you learned?"

"Other than that Mariel Marsden has an irrational animosity toward you, not a great deal." Giles hesitated. "You will not like to hear this, but—"

From the doorway, Tidcombe intoned, "The Dowager Countess of Dorset." Hannah swept into the room.

She stopped short at sight of Giles. "Lud. I have interrupted a tête-à-tête."

"Nothing of the sort," Giles responded smoothly. "We have been discussing a business matter. I was about to leave." He bowed. "Lady Clea. We will speak of this again."

What had he been about to tell her? Of a certainty they would speak again, and soon. "I look forward to it," Clea said politely. "Coward," she hissed, under her breath.

He winked at her, but made no reply.

"Lawrence is quite wealthy," Hannah observed after the door had closed behind him. "The man has no title, and a murky background, but he is eligible nonetheless. You could do worse. You *will* do worse if you do not curtail your rash behavior. I hear you and Baron Saxe are wondrous great together. Clea, it will not serve."

Clea recalled her last encounter with the baron. Wondrous great together? Hannah had no idea.

"Well?" the dowager demanded. "Have you nothing to say for yourself?"

The things Clea was tempted to say, her cousin would not care to hear. "You make too much of it. I've known Kane since I was a child."

"You are no longer a child," snapped Hannah. "It's time you stopped acting as if you were. I tried my best to teach you how you should go on, but obviously I failed. Now we must all suffer the consequences of your actions. It is more than a person should be expected to bear."

Clea was startled to see the dowager's cheeks turn an alarming shade of purple. "Don't put yourself in a taking, cousin. I am not as bad as that."

"Are you not?" Hannah marched up to the desk, snatched up the little pistol. "I *should* shoot you! It would save the family a great deal of fuss."

Chapter Twenty-Five

A man's character is his fate. — Heraclitus

Kane stormed through the front door of the Academy and into the marble-tiled entry. "Where is she?" he demanded of the footman who sought to bar his path.

The servant flinched, but stood his ground. "If you care to wait in the sitting room, my lord, I'll inform the mistress that you're here."

Lilah had been expecting him, and well she might. She should be grateful he'd delayed calling on her until he regained a degree of self-control. Kane stalked down the hallway and up the stairs.

He entered the sitting room. A recent conversation with Amory Marsden had not improved his mood, Mr. Marsden having suggested that long acquaintance with Clea had blinded Kane to her deficiencies of character. Kane had in turn informed Mr. Marsden that people who dwelt in glass houses, or in this instance had murderously-inclined mamas, should refrain from hurling aspersions. Amory admitted stiffly that his mother was prejudiced against Clea, but refused to believe that she would act on her emotions. The men had not parted on good terms.

Kane picked up a decanter, splashed whisky into a glass. He was angry with Amory, Lilah, Clea, and numerous members of the government, up to and including the King.

Above all, Kane was furious with himself.

He had taken advantage of Clea. Or she had taken advantage of him. Kane was uncertain which of them was the most culpable at this point.

Lilah entered the room. She was every inch the lady of the manor today, in a prim silk gown that matched her eyes.

She looked him over, coolly. "Have you come to cross swords with me, my lord? You must have known that I would speak with your friend should she choose to pursue the acquaintance. Since you failed to convince her that she should *not* pursue the acquaintance, you may only blame yourself."

Kane bit back a sharp retort. What Lilah said was true. He had failed to convince Clea that she should not rub shoulders with fallen women.

With this particular fallen woman.

Had Lilah not been his mistress, would Clea have been so prompt to seek her out?

Kane swallowed a sip of whisky. In addition to his other failings of character, he had apparently developed an exaggerated notion of his own worth. "Hell and the devil confound it," he said.

Lilah settled on her loveseat. "Lady Clea complimented me on my well-trained servants. She seemed surprised *they* weren't surprised to find a lady lurking at my kitchen door."

Clea had no notion how well-trained Lilah's servants were. At least, Kane hoped Clea had not.

"You will be wondering why she came to see me," Lilah continued. "Lady Clea was anxious to discover if Viscount Carruthers had engaged in post-coital confidences. I told her he had not."

What Kane was wondering was if Clea grew loose-tongued after love-making. Incorrigible reprobate that he was.

Had Lilah told Clea the truth? Would she tell *him* the truth if he posed her the same question? "Since we are on the subject, you know of no reason why Carruthers might have been murdered?" he asked.

Lilah shook her head. "Does there need to be a reason? London is a dangerous city. His death may have been a random act. In any event, I'm not the person to ask. Carnal acquaintance aside, I barely knew the man. As I also told Lady Clea, I hardly cherish tender sentiments toward every man who has shared my bed."

Kane winced. That Lilah had feelings for him, he knew. The nature of those feelings, he could but guess. She had showed scant reaction when she saw him sprawled on her loveseat, fondling Clea's breast.

That same loveseat where she currently sat.

"Clea told me Mariel Marsden visited your shop," he said. "Why did she not go to an apothecary instead?"

Lilah arched an ironic eyebrow. "No legitimate apothecary would make up a potion as strong as she requested. I do have a certain reputation, deserved or no."

So she did. It was common knowledge in certain circles that the Temple of Beauty hired out rooms for private rendezvous. Less widely known was the fact that the establishment's owner occasionally supplied stimulation for well-born ladies who sought rather more excitement than usually found in the marriage bed. Kane said, "Aphrodisiacs are one thing, poisons another. Surely she did not ask you for poison outright?"

"Mrs. Marsden did not ask me for anything, but spoke with my representative." Lilah folded her hands in her lap. "You may not be aware of the diverse elements involved in the preparation of cosmetics. If my clients were made aware of the ingredients I use, they might not be as eager to slather my costly concoctions on their faces and elsewhere. Or maybe they would. My ladies are generally being too wrapped up in their own reflections to care if a preparation contains arsenic or slaked lime."

Kane experienced a surge of irritation. He was in no mood to hear, for example, that a certain noted actress slept nightly plastered with a paste made of egg whites, alum and sweet almonds spread on a muslin mask. But Lilah added, merely, "If ever I *were* inclined to provide a client with a killing potion, I would have sufficient ingredients available to me. Mrs. Marsden failed to take into consideration the fact that I am a businesswoman. There is little profit in being hanged."

Kane was glad to hear her say it. "What, exactly, *did* Mariel Marsden request?"

"A sleeping potion strong enough that she might slumber through Armageddon. The woman has taken laudanum so long that normal doses have no effect, or so she explained to my representative, who grew immediately suspicious and contacted me. Specialized formulations are not made on the shop premises, but by a chemist whom I employ. Mrs. Marsden was instructed to return for her purchase later in the week."

Kane refrained from inquiring about the nature of those 'specialized formulations'. "You should have informed me at once."

She looked amused. "For what purpose, pray? This is hardly the first time I have received such a request. If I may continue: what Mrs. Marsden took away with her is basically a tincture of opium, with a few additional ingredients. A person would have to swallow the entire bottle to do lasting damage, and the taste is sufficiently vile that no one could stomach such a great amount. Mrs. Marsden will be displeased when she realizes that the draught will not serve her purpose — providing she drums up sufficient courage to go through with the thing, which I take leave to doubt."

Kane was less certain. "Yet you gave Clea an antidote."

Lilah sighed. "Pray don't be dense. I gave Lady Clea a warning. And before you ask why I involved myself, I will tell you that I cannot help but admire a female who makes it so obvious that she finds propriety a dead bore."

'Dead', Kane reflected sourly, was all too appropriate a word.

Lilah patted the loveseat. "Come, let us talk of happier things. I have arranged a re-enactment of the various seductions of Zeus. Perhaps you would like to attend."

Satyr, swan, ant, pigeon and golden shower— Kane could conceive of little he would like less.

Although, as concerned the latter, he was mildly intrigued.

He might have joined Lilah, had she been seated somewhere else, had he not recalled the last time he sat on that loveseat, with Clea pressed against him, her heart racing beneath his palm.

He stayed where he was.

Lilah cocked her head to one side. "I believe I will invite Lady Clea to one of our amusements. She might be amused."

Amused? By an orgy? "You—"

Lilah pursed her lips. "Shall we resort to name-calling? In that case: sneaksby. Bully. Babblemouth."

He *should* lock Clea in the turret room. Maybe he would lock himself in with her, and leave the rest of the world to go hang. "You failed to mention beef-wit and prude."

"Oh, my dear," Lilah said softly. "You're in love with her."

Carefully Kane put down his glass. "To whom do you refer? Mariel Marsden? The Queen?"

Lilah lifted one hand, let it fall. "Be that as it may, or not, I have recently become aware of rumors that may concern you. Gentlemen gossip as much as their female counterparts, as you well know. Currently they are whispering that Harry Marsden shot himself because he caught his wife *in flagrante delicto* with another man — and not for the first time."

Chapter Twenty-Six

Very few things happen at the right time, and the rest do not happen at all. — Herodotus

Late afternoon sunlight filtered through the turret room's clouded window-glass. Pilar finished tying back the draperies and brushed dust off her hands. "*Não há duas sem trôs,*" she said pointedly. "There is no two without a three."

Quando o bem te chegar, mete-o em casa, thought Clea. Opportunity knocks only once. She approached the daybed where Fausto, having just dispatched an imprudent mouse, was curled up with its corpse on Francis Wakely's black velvet cloak; scooped up the limp rodent body and dropped it out an open window. "Cry pax, Pilar. I can take care of myself."

The senhora folded her arms beneath her magnificent bosom, set off today by Pomona green and jonquil stripes. "*Sim.* You've done such a good job of it thus far."

Frankie, who had been following the conversation with interest, ventured an opinion that Pilar shouldn't be surprised by anything Lady Clea did. "A gentry mort with brass enough to shoot a shaffle ain't like to think twice about visiting a bawdyken."

"Shaffle?" Pilar echoed.

"A highwayman," Clea explained. "A smashing cove is a housebreaker, a spicer is a footpad." She glanced at Frankie, who was sitting stiffly in the carved chair, looking vastly uncomfortable in the borrowed chintz gown that had been supplied as a substitute for breeches in hope that, should she attempt an escape, a dress would slow her down. "And knuckles are superior practitioners of the pocket-picking art."

Frankie smirked.

"On the contrary," Pilar protested. "I am not scolding because Clea went to visit a female of low reputation—"

"Which is a good thing," put in Clea, "because in that event I would be compelled to point out that your own reputation has not benefitted from association with a certain *bandido.*"

"Experience is the mother of wisdom. Therefore I know of which I speak. As I was saying, I am cross not because of where you went — although it is monstrous *fatiguing* when you do not think before you act — but because you did not take the appropriate precautions. If you will recall—" Pilar lifted one finger, a second, a third. "The female in the Chiado fruit market. The man you shoved overboard. The intruder at the inn. The highwayman. Bow Street. Berkley Square."

"Lawks!" commented Frankie. "Sounds like it's *you* who should be laying low."

Clea overlooked this interruption. "Yet here I am, relatively unscathed."

Pilar flung both hands in the air. "*Deus!* You are exceedingly pig-headed. I regret that I left Portugal."

"You left Portugal because you wanted to teach Don Miguel a much-needed lesson. Or so you said at the time." Clea returned to the daybed, reached down to stroke the cat. Fausto belched, emitting rodent breath, and batted her hand away.

Frankie snickered. Clea scowled. Frankie lowered her gaze to the stiffly jointed wooden doll she cradled in her lap.

Pilar claimed someone had rifled through her belongings. Clea had been skeptical at the time. Lately, however, she had begun to suspect that someone had been rummaging through her room, in spite of her locked door.

Searching for a certain notebook, mayhap?

Had Frankie had managed to sneak out of the turret room?

The girl touched one tentative finger to the doll's painted face.

They would be hard-pressed to keep those clever fingers away from anything she could filch or pawn.

What *was* to be done with her?

More to the point, what was to be done with Harry's mysterious notebook? For all the sense Clea could make of it, the thing might have been written in Greek.

She could pay a visit to Croyden. But Clea no more dared show the notebook to Colonel Scoville than she dared show it to Ned.

She might as well be in possession of an unexploded artillery shell.

Frankie peered up at the painting hanging on the chimney wall. "I'll wager that dimber chappy had a cheese-toaster," she said.

Clea glanced at the portrait. Francis Wakefield *had* possessed a smallsword. She didn't like to remember how it had got lost.

"You may have your knife back when you leave us," she told Frankie. "But if you pike off now, you're like to have *your* throat slit, so stow your gaff. Which reminds me, what did you do with the little Spanish pistol you filched from me?"

Frankie sniffed. "Hocked it o' course. Brought me a pretty penny, it did."

Clea abandoned all hope of retrieving Harry's gift. "You haven't explained why you were following me."

"Because you was acting beetle-headed stupid," Frankie replied.

"Ask me no questions, in other words," said Pilar, "and I'll tell you no taradiddles. You were an excellent, ah, picker of pockets, Frankie, yes?"

Frankie jerked her head at Clea. "Picked *her* pocket, didn't I?"

"You snatched my purse out of my hand," protested Clea. "That is an altogether different thing."

The girl was pale, she realized. Frankie's rigid posture was due not only to wearing an unfamiliar corset, but result of having had a knife jabbed in her ribs.

She remembered Giles and his blasted proverb. 'If you save someone's life...' Had Clea saved Frankie's life, or had Frankie saved hers? Hard to say which debt would be the most cumbersome.

What had Giles been about to say when Hannah interrupted? And what had put the dowager in such a temper that she threatened to shoot her cousin, an act that seemed to shock her even more than it had Clea; immediately thereafter Hannah had issued one last warning about what became of heedless young women who flouted society's rules and departed the room as hastily as if she feared her own correctness might be compromised.

A woman's honor lay in public recognition of her virtue, a man's in the reliability of his word. Kit Graham had led Clea to Bow Street and abandoned her there, proving himself unreliable indeed.

Such behavior didn't fit with the man Clea had once known.

Frankie and Pilar had put their heads together over a newspaper. Ignoring Clea's reservations, Pilar was helping Frankie to develop her reading skills.

Clea looked again at the portrait. What would Francis Wakely have made of the current political hullabaloo?

Probably it would have amused him, heedless profligate that he had been.

A profligate who died insane and pox'd, his mocking face eaten half away.

She refused to think of Kane.

For one startled second, it seemed as if Francis Wakely winked at her.

Footsteps sounded on the stairway. Had they been found out? Everyone turned to look at the door.

A small slender female with a heart-shaped face stepped across the threshold. She was dressed for travelling in a carriage gown of jaconet muslin and a pretty figured spencer. Guinea-gold curls peered out from beneath the brim of a bonnet adorned with a bunch of exotic flowers at the front.

Bright blue eyes inspected the startled faces turned toward her. "Hullo, Clea. Welcome home."

Chapter Twenty-Seven

*Today's today. Tomorrow we may be ourselves gone down
the drain of eternity. — Euripides*

Frankie stared at the tall auburn-haired man standing in the doorway. "I'm Ned Fairchild, owner of this fine edifice," he explained. "And this is Lady Dorset, my wife. Julie, I'd like you to meet Senhora Pilar Estevez. She is an old friend."

"Pleased, I'm sure." Pulling off her bonnet, the blue-eyed woman sat down beside Lady Clea on the daybed.

Pilar clapped her hands together. "Welcome, milady! I am glad you're here. Maybe you can convince Clea that she does not have as many lives as a cat."

The earl frowned at his sister. "I thought we agreed you would take precautions, puss."

"I promised nothing," Clea protested. "You merely decreed."

"That's the way it is with the nobs. They get in the habit of giving orders." Lady Dorset nudged Fausto aside so she might curl up beside him on the velvet cloak.

"Some of the luckier ones," her husband observed, "even have their orders obeyed."

His countess grinned.

Frankie was so fascinated she almost forgot the corset jabbing into her sore ribs. Lady Dorset was famous among her fellow filchers, having been the cleverest of conveyancers until she'd run afoul of one of the swell mob and wound up shackled to an earl.

What would Earlene have made of all this?

Earlene would have told Frankie to keep her peepers peeled, that's what.

"Your pig-headed sister went to visit Lilah Kingston," Pilar informed the earl. "Baron Saxe fetched her home. This was after our little pocket-picker here was damaged coming to Clea's aid when ruffians tried to snatch her up in Bow Street." Lord Dorset's vivid green gaze rested speculatively on Frankie. She fought back an urge to squirm.

"I meant to speak with Carruthers," Clea explained. "Someone apparently preferred that I did not."

The earl turned back to her. "Has this to do with Harry?" he asked.

Clea sighed, "I wish I knew."

Frankie's ears perked up. Who was this Harry gent?

"Cousin Hannah threatened to shoot me," Clea added. "I have no notion why."

"I do," murmured Pilar.

The earl smiled at his wife. "Now that we have come back to town, Hannah will expect you to keep Clea in line."

"And so I shall, when hens grow teeth." The countess reached for the plate abandoned on the daybed, picked up a crumb of cheese and popped it into her mouth.

The small room was crowded with so many people in it. Frankie eyed the doorway, which the earl was blocking, and after it the window — through which at the rate she was stuffing her belly with the food her captors smuggled to the attic, she soon wouldn't fit — and contemplated her chances of escape.

Lady Dorset wriggled her bottom further back among the pillows. Annoyed at having his rest disturbed, Fausto jumped down and began to savage the bonnet she'd tossed onto the floor.

"Naughty cat!" Pilar scolded, as she scooped up her pet.

"I have other bonnets," the countess said indifferently, for all the world as if she hadn't herself not long ago reckoned to a tuppence what such an item might fetch in a Two-to-One shop; the countess who was not only the wife of an earl and the granddaughter of a marquess but had also spent time in quod before a certain Bow Street Runner got her out. Frankie said abruptly, "Pritchett calls you 'Jules'."

"I shan't tell you what I call Pritchett." Lady Dorset kicked off her lilac slippers and tucked her feet up under her skirts. "More to the point, what are we to call *you*?"

"Kane told us her name is Frankie," Clea said.

The countess rolled her eyes. "And if Kane tells us something, we must accept it as God's truth."

Oho. Lady Dorset was no admirer of Lord Saxe. Frankie pondered how that circumstance might be put to the best use.

"Frankie it is," conceded the countess. "You're the nibbler who filched Clea's reticule. I'll warrant you can draw a thimble or a wiper as easy as pissing the bed."

Pilar looked startled. "*O que?*"

The earl leaned one broad shoulder against the wall by the closed door. "My wife is demonstrating that she can still talk flash."

"Speak Greek," Clea explained helpfully. "Rum patter. Slang. Frankie had a pocket watch in her possession when we brought her here. We would return it to its rightful owner if we knew who that was."

"That ticker's mine," Frankie protested. "Left me by me old da' when he stuck his spoon in the wall."

"Your old da' had a gold watch? Tell us another," Clea scoffed.

"Possession is nine-tenths of the law," Lady Dorset pointed out.

"In that case," Clea concluded, "the watch belongs to me."

"And you call *me* a thief!" Frankie cried indignantly.

The countess scooped up another crumb from the tray. Pilar crossed to the window, Fausto clasped firmly in her arms.

Lord Dorset pushed himself away from the wall. "Who set you to spying on my sister, Frankie? Don't insult my intelligence by spinning me a Canterbury tale."

Frankie marveled at herself. From sleeping amongst the rotting garbage of the Covent Garden stalls to flimflamming a lordship in his own attics: how she'd risen in the world. "I wasn't spying on anyone. Seems to me this is a fine thankee for me stopping Lady Clea from being snatched."

"Seems to *me* that whatever you did, you did because it suited your purpose," the countess remarked.

Lord Dorset stepped forward. Frankie squelched a cowardly impulse to shrink back in her chair. He grasped her chin in his strong fingers, held her so firmly that she couldn't turn away. "You had in your possession a Spanish folding knife. Why didn't you use your weapon when you came to my sister's defense?"

Frankie snorted. "Why didn't I waltz up to the hangman and stick my head in his noose? Which is what would happen if someone like me poked a hole in a gentry cove."

The earl released her and stepped back. "A gentry cove. Are you sure?"

"As sure as I know chalk from cheese."

"And doesn't *that* make a person sit up and take notice?" the countess remarked. "My husband finds himself in a bit of a dilemma, Frankie. You did come to Clea's aid. At the same time, Ned doesn't trust your motives and would like to give you a good shake."

Frankie hoped 'Ned' wouldn't try it, because then she'd have to kick *him* in the twiddle-diddles, as result of which he'd have her out the window, whether she fit or no.

The earl ran his eyes over her, like she was a bug he had skewered on a pin. Frankie felt like telling his high-and-mightiness that he might take himself to blazes, but before she could he smiled — a genuine, charming, rascally sort of smile — and all her angry thoughts flew right out of her head.

"I don't know what rig you're running," he admitted. "Though I'm sure you're running one. But as my wife reminds me, it seems unlikely you mean Clea any real harm. If you agree to temporarily set aside your purpose in preference for ours, I'll promise to see you safe when you're done playing least-in-sight."

"We have a purpose?" echoed Clea. "I wish you would tell me what it is."

"Yes, do!" agreed Pilar.

Lord Dorset's attention remained fixed on Frankie. "First I must have her word."

Frankie shifted, felt the prickle of the paper she'd stuffed under her stays. The note she'd found tucked up amidst the old Italian playing cards. How it had got there, she couldn't begin to guess.

But she took its meaning plain enough.

If the earl had a plan, she'd best discover what that plan was. "Done," Frankie said.

Lady Dorset swung her feet to the floor, walked to Frankie's chair. She spat into her palm.

Frankie blinked, stood, and spat into her own. They clasped hands, and shook. "Break faith," the countess muttered, "and I'll have your guts for fiddle-strings."

Chapter Twenty-Eight

*A happy life is one which is in accordance with its own
nature. — Seneca*

The evening was damp and foggy, the hour considerably advanced
when Baron Saxe and Lord Dorset mounted the stairs to White's.
"You'd trust the word of a purse snatcher?" Kane asked skeptically.

Ned surrendered his hat to the doorman. "I trust our little Tyburn
blossom knows which side her bread is buttered on."

He sounded certain. Kane, who didn't share Ned's soft spot for
gutterpups, was considerably less so.

Both men were dressed for evening in knee-breeches and long-
tailed coats and starched cravats. They had just come from Drury Lane,
where the family had enjoyed a production featuring the particular
friend of Julie's grandfather, the marquess.

"Just what *is* this plan of yours?" Kane persisted, as the men
strolled through the club rooms.

"I haven't quite decided," the earl admitted. "I'll let you know as
soon as I've settled the details."

Kane was to be permitted no part in the arrangements? He bit
back a snarl.

White's was, as usual, crowded at this hour. Lord Saxe and the Earl
of Dorset attracted no little notice as they passed through the
overheated rooms. The baron knew everyone worth knowing, and a
great many others who were not, and was consequently *au courant*
with the latest turns of events, political and otherwise; the earl was a
source of constant speculation among the *haut ton*, due to his

disinclination to behave as they expected, not to mention the stigma of having been one of Wellington's spies.

Ignoring the curious glances cast in their direction, Kane accepted a glass of claret from a waiter. "You think to find your villains here?"

"I'm fairly certain I won't find them at Wakely Court." Ned paused to watch a game of billiards. Made aware of his interest, one of the players missed his shot.

The return of Lord Dorset to London was not the only, or even the main, topic of conversation at White's that evening. General conversation centered on the Queen's fate, Brougham having proclaimed that he could and would proceed no further when he discovered that a witness had been prevented from coming to testify in Princess Caroline's defense.

"The imagination boggles," marveled Ned, word of these latest developments not having reached the wilds of Sussex before he and Julie left for town.

Kane did not respond, having spied Amory Marsden in the card room, seated with several other men around a table, engaged in a not-very-serious hand of whist. On glimpsing Kane, Amory threw down his cards and pushed back his chair.

"What is your opinion of this latest development, Saxe?" he asked as he approached them. "Do you agree with Holland that even if the Milan Commission acted improperly, more than sufficient evidence of Caroline's misconduct exists?"

Unlike Amory, Kane felt no need to present an impression of polite conversation to their avid audience. He said, bluntly, "I've had no stomach for the business from the start."

Ned stepped between them. "I understand you've called in Bow Street to investigate your brother's death, Marsden. Interesting that you should have so little concern about hanging your family's dirty linen out to air."

Amory's expression, as he looked at the earl, was that of a man who'd bitten into something sour. "Speaking of dirty laundry, have you heard the latest rumors concerning your sister? Do us all a favor. Remove her from town." Abandoning any pretense of politeness, Amory turned on his heel and walked away.

"I don't know why people think I have such great influence with Clea," Ned remarked. "What recent rumors was Marsden talking about?"

Kane wished himself elsewhere, anywhere that he wouldn't be required to have this conversation. "Gossip claims Clea had a lover, or lovers, and that's why Harry Marsden shot himself. I had it from Lilah. Where Lilah heard it, I don't know."

Ned strode silently through the club rooms to the front hallway, where he reclaimed his hat.

Kane followed his friend outside. "I take it you've had enough of White's. Where are we going now?"

"To speak with Mrs. Kingston. Concerning this rumor she's helping put about."

The foggy streets were thronged with horses and carriages and liveried servants, less fortunate pedestrians scurrying to avoid being crushed under the wheels of gentlefolk traveling from one entertainment to another. The men set out on foot, the Academy not being far from White's.

"You know that Clea visited Lilah?" Kane asked his friend.

"I do," said Ned. "Suspecting that you already had Clea's head for washing, I refrained from making my own feelings known. Did you set spies on her? I daresay Clea had *your* head for washing about that."

So Clea had. She'd called Kane several unflattering names.

After he'd accused her of lacking the sense God gave a goose.

King's Place was lined with carriages. Music drifted out on the damp night air. The windows of the Academy blazed with light. "Tell your mistress that Lord Dorset would like a word," Kane instructed the servant who opened the front door.

"Yes, my lord," the servant replied. "If you will come with me—"

The public rooms were overflowing, lending credence to Lilah's claim that every one of White's five hundred members had at one time or another crossed her threshold, sometimes several together, which wasn't meant to suggest that the members of Brook's and Boodles' took their pleasure elsewhere.

In the upper hallway, relative quiet reigned. The footman opened the door to Lilah's sitting room, indicated that the men should enter, closed the door behind them. Ned approached the mahogany sideboard with the ease of long acquaintance, picked up a decanter, poured liquor into a glass. "You may give me your congratulations. Julie is *enceinte*. We shan't tell Hannah just yet that a Dorset heir is in the offing, lest she start fussing like a hen with one chick."

No little bit appalled, Kane managed, "I trust your wife is in good health."

"That depends on who you ask. The medic says so, but Julie will inform you that she is suffering fatigue, headaches, back pain and a tendency to cast up her accounts. Too, she is changeable as a weathercock. One minute we're merry as crickets, and the next she vows she will die of the dumps. I fear she is not enjoying the experience overmuch."

Kane immediately resolved to stay as far as possible out of Julie's way.

Lilah entered the room, clad in a low-cut corseted costume and tall boots, a parrot on her shoulder and a cutlass at her hip. She held out her hands to the earl. "Welcome, Ned. I hope you have not come to scold me for entertaining your sister. Kane has already made it clear that he does not approve."

Her tone was teasing. The parrot nibbled at her ear. Kane puzzled over what part the bird might be assigned in tonight's debaucheries.

The imagination boggled, indeed.

Ned clasped Lilah's hands, released them. "I've come not to scold, but beg a favor. I hope that you will tell me— This current rumor concerning Clea, who did you have it from?"

Lilah shrugged, causing the parrot to mutter darkly. "One hears all manner of rumors in a brothel. It is difficult to pinpoint the source."

"You led me to conclude that a man lay behind it," Kane reminded her. " 'Gentlemen gossip as much as their female counterparts' were your exact words."

Lilah raised one hand to soothe the bird. "I said that? Your memory is better than mine. Still, considering the nature of this house, odds are that the speaker was in fact male." She glanced from Kane to Ned. "In any event, I don't believe for an instant that your sister is the sort of woman who would play her husband false. Any more than you are the sort of man who would betray his wife."

Ned smiled as easily as if her words held no hidden meaning. "And so I would not."

Kane wondered what the earl saw when he looked at Lilah. A beautiful woman or a shrewd, manipulative courtesan far past her first youth?

Unfair, he told himself. Lilah was as she had always been. It was he who had changed.

His gaze drifted to the loveseat. He hadn't seen Clea since he last met her in this room. When Clea had demanded that he kiss her properly, and he had obliged.

Maybe he should take himself off to Antarctica and live among the penguins. If the cold didn't kill his ardor, it might at least freeze off his stones.

Ned said, sounding puzzled, "Kane?"

Kane realized he was scowling at the loveseat. He had a horrified suspicion that Lilah might have mentioned finding him there with Clea on his lap. In which case Ned would either shoot him, or he would have to blow out his own brains.

Like Harry Marsden had done. Or not. Kane winced.

Lilah shot him a knowing glance. "If that is all, gentlemen? I must return to my guests. Tonight we are staging an amatory amusement with pirates — semi-anonymous encounters in tents erected on an imitation ship's deck — in honor of the Queen."

Chapter Twenty-Nine

In war there is no prize for runner-up. — Seneca

"*Quem não quer ser lobo nao lhe vista a pele,*" observed Senhora Estevez. "He who doesn't want to be a wolf shouldn't wear its hide, and therefore I make myself as unobtrusive as a mouse. We are having an adventure, and I appreciate a good adventure, providing I am not required to tire myself." She pinched Clea's arm. "Also providing that, during this adventure, you do not get yourself dispatched."

Clea, too, hoped that she might not. Her attempt to attract no particular attention involved a green sarcenet pelisse and white muslin walking dress; a simple straw bonnet with a cylindrical crown, tied with a ribbon under her chin; half-boots of kid. Pilar's notion of unremarkable, however, included an Indian shawl made into a dress, its border forming the hemline; a Spanish pelisse of shot sarsenet trimmed with Egyptian crape and Chinese binding; lemon kid gloves and slippers; a narrow brimmed bonnet trimmed with ribbon, lace, and a jaunty plume.

The coffee house outside which they stood being unobtrusive was much like any other. Pedestrians and street sellers hurried past. Carts and drays and private carriages jostled for position in the narrow noisy streets.

A hackney coach, drawn by two horses, drew up beside them; a closed, four-wheeled bumbling vehicle with small shuttered windows, painted a nondescript brown. The door swung open. A hand beckoned them within.

Clea hesitated. Pilar nudged her. Clea squared her shoulders and mounted the step.

The interior of the coach was no more prepossessing than its exterior, the upholstery worn and stained. Clea's eyes rested first on Giles Lawrence, whom she had not expected, then on his companion, a tall, fit gentleman with brown hair and finely sculpted features and an impressive beak of a nose, dressed for riding in a blue coat with brass buttons, leather breeches and top boots. His expression was impatient, as if he was so pressed for time he might at any moment bolt out the door.

Clea imagined he *was* pressed for time, this man whom Tsar Alexander of Russia called 'the conqueror of the world's conqueror'; and the newssheets called 'Old Nosey'; and whose officers called him 'the Beau'.

"Boa tarde, meu senhor Duque." Pilar settled on the seat beside Clea. *"Como vai?"*

He rapped on the ceiling, signaling the driver to move on. "I am the better for seeing you, Senhora Estevez."

Some things, Clea mused, did not change with time. *Ce cher Villainton,* as the noted Italian contralto Giuseppina Grassini had dubbed him, still had an eye for a pretty, witty female.

La Grassini had been mistress of both Napoleon and Wellington, though not at the same time. The duke had not only acquired two of Napoleon's mistresses, he had bought Napoleon's sister's home, called upon Napoleon's sister-in-law, and engaged Napoleon's cook.

Clea had last spoken with Wellington in Vienna, when all the world was gay and she was in love with Harry, before the Corsican's escape from Elba had plunged them back into war. "Your Grace. It is good of you to make time for me," she said.

His cool gaze rested on her, those eyes that in some light were blue and in others grey, and had inspired more than one subaltern to quake in his boots. "I'd a great deal rather take time for you than some of the people I'm currently dealing with," he remarked.

Clea didn't doubt it. The hero of Waterloo was no longer as universally beloved as once he had been. These days, crowds tended to greet Wellington's arrival not with cheers but hisses and shouts and waved fists. To add insult to injury, when reporting to the King on proceedings in the Commons, the duke had been commanded to hold his tongue.

She felt the outline of the little pistol resting in her reticule. "You will have heard of Harry's death."

Wellington's stern features softened. "Yes, and I am sorry for it. He was a good man. Lawrence tells me you're bent on stirring up a hornet's nest, my girl."

Clea glanced at Giles, who had the grace to look abashed. He wore a tightly-fitting coat of superfine today, a buff colored waistcoat and deep stiff cravat, fawn pantaloons and Hessian boots.

"This is a bad business," the duke added, "and your meddling has made it worse. You don't accept that Harry shot himself? Nor do I. But you must stand back now and let others deal with the matter. We are not ready to flush out our fox."

Pilar had been uncharacteristically silent, perhaps recalling the days when thieves were prone to cut through the back of hackney coaches and snatch passenger's wigs off their heads. "There is a fox?"

"So it would seem. Unfortunately, I am as yet uncertain of his identity." Wellington turned back to Clea. "I *am* certain it wasn't your Harry, though I'm not prepared to make that statement publicly."

At last, someone believed her. Clea clutched the seat as the coach made an especially sharp turn.

His suspicions had first been roused, Wellington explained — after an anxious moment when it was unclear whether the vehicle would right itself — when Marmont came rampaging in to relieve Ciudad Rodrigo and caught him, through a rare failure to concentrate, with his army dangerously strung out. He had become even more suspicious when an error of judgment caused him to mislead Blücher into making a stand at Ligny that resulted in a Prussian defeat. Later, at the Duchess of Richmond's ball in Brussels, the night before the Battle of Quatre Bras, he had learned that Napoleon was attacking not on the west as expected but on the Allied army's eastern flank.

In other words, Clea concluded, the duke had been humbugged.

"You haven't," Giles reminded him, "mentioned Badajoz."

Wellington looked annoyed.

Clea frowned. Badajoz lay just inside the Spanish border. Five thousand British and Portuguese soldiers had died there, and another four thousand civilians when the victorious troops sacked the town. Even more than their cousin's inconvenient death, the battle of Badajoz and its aftermath had caused Ned to end his military career. "I don't understand. What has Harry's death to do with Badajoz?"

Wellington did not reply.

"Clea is having far too many 'accidents', sir," Giles continued. "Someone thinks she knows more than she does. Or more than she is admitting, at any rate."

"*Santo Deus!*" sighed Pilar.

Wellington said, stiffly, "Clea's involvement is unfortunate. All the same, our traitor must be caught and held to account."

Did Wellington consider Harry's death 'unfortunate'? Clea wondered. Were they nothing more than pawns to be moved about willy-nilly on the duke's chessboard? "What is it someone thinks I know?"

Wellington said, with obvious reluctance, "In the confusion following the battle of Badajoz, a considerable amount of gold was stolen from the Fortress. The Portuguese government would like to have it back."

And, for obvious reasons, the British government was anxious to avoid further public embarrassment. "And Harry knew of this?" Clea asked.

"Harry knew I suspected a traitor," the Duke told her. "Nothing more. Unfortunately, we have no way of determining what else he may have found out."

Clea decided not to mention a certain little notebook. "I take it that I'm interfering with your plans."

The Duke didn't deny it. "Lawrence is convinced you won't be persuaded to depart London. If that is true, I must insist that you leave this matter to older, wiser heads."

Wellington was accustomed to commanding armies, issuing orders so clearly and concisely they could not be misunderstood. At the moment, he was commanding Clea. "And if I don't agree?"

He looked at her down his long nose. "I daresay you would prefer your brother does not become involved."

Did Wellington expect that on his command Ned would give her a tongue-lashing? Confine her to starvation rations in her room? If so, he was far off the mark. Clea's brother had last attempted to discipline her when she was five years old, an undertaking that had left him so shaken she'd ended up comforting them both.

Not being of a mind to cut off her nose to spite her face, Clea said, "I understand."

"I am glad to hear it." The duke rapped on the carriage roof. "This conversation will remain between ourselves."

The carriage drew to a halt. He nodded. "Good day, Lady Clea. Senhora Estevez." Giles opened the door.

The street was even busier than they'd left it. Pilar peered at the coffee house and announced herself possessed of a great thirst. Clea followed her friend into a large, crowded room.

The walls were wainscoted, the ceilings beamed, the wooden floor scuffed. Earthenware jars with Dutch scenes of windmills and fishing boats rested on the fireplace mantle, alongside blue and white pottery plates painted with landscapes, seascapes, hunting scenes. Pint coffeepots waited ready by the antique grate. Advertisements for patent medicines adorned the walls.

A harried waiter led them to a table. Clea gazed curiously around, having not previously visited a coffee house that catered exclusively to her own sex. Women of all shapes and stations were perusing the latest newspapers, conversing about politics, scandals, philosophy. The shrill cacophony of female voices made Clea wince.

The waiter returned, placed two cups of steaming coffee in shallow delftware bowls and a plate bearing several slices of almond cake on the table, then scurried away.

Clea picked up her cup. "Well. I've been put in my place."

"Dogs bark, but the caravan moves on, *querida*." Pilar plunged her fork into a piece of cake.

Chapter Thirty

*He who is of a calm and happy nature, will hardly feel the
pressure of age. — Plato*

Lord Saxe squinted up at Wakely Court's eccentric skyline. The chimney pots seemed to sway gently in the breeze, their bizarre behavior proof — had he needed proof — of his latest debauch.

The evening had begun, as had so many recently, with a social gathering and the inevitable political disputations, most notably a discussion of royal prerogative that became confused with the concept of divine right. Few who spoke on these subjects had any clear understanding of them yet they still had much to say, as result of which Kane had consumed a great deal more liquor than was wise. He'd staggered home to, instead of sinking as he'd hoped into a dreamless slumber, lay awake staring at the ceiling until at last he'd got up and gone to the Academy, where he engaged himself counting harlots as opposed to sheep.

He'd no more desire to embrace one than the other.

The ramifications of that realization, he chose to ignore.

Tidcombe met him in the hallway. "Good afternoon, my lord. The master is in the library. The ladies have gone out."

Kane understood from this remark that the butler approved of neither his master, the ladies, nor the library itself. "Out? Where did they go?"

Recited Tidcombe, woodenly, "I'm sure I couldn't say."

Couldn't, perhaps, and probably wouldn't even if he could. Kane handed the butler his hat and gloves. "Don't disturb yourself,

Tidcombe. I know the way."

Lord Dorset was, as promised, in the library, the *Cryptology* open on the desk in front of him, Fausto stretched across his lap.

The cat looked up as Kane entered. So did Ned. The earl's auburn hair was tousled, as if he'd run restless fingers through it, giving him less the appearance of an indolent nobleman than the adventurer he'd been not long ago.

"The lawyers are displaying their eloquence," Kane informed his friend as he dropped into a chair. "Thomas Denman summed up the defense. He likened the King's treatment of the Queen to that of Nero and Octavia. In his closing speech he urged mercy, and ended with the words 'Go and sin no more,' which I imagine he already regrets."

"One of the penalties for refusing to engage in politics is that you end up being governed by your inferiors," remarked the earl. "Plato said that, I believe. Would you like something to drink?"

At thought of alcohol, Kane grimaced. "Thank you, I would not. Plato said a great many things, among them that wise men speak because they have something to say, while fools speak because they have to say something. Why am I here?"

Ned gestured toward the handwritten notes spread out in front of him on the desk. "Harry Marsden had in his possession a partly coded ledger. Clea discovered it in his trunk. She has been trying to decipher it. These are her notes."

Kane found in his friend's remarks several causes for both annoyance and alarm, not least the fact that Clea hadn't seen fit to inform him the notebook existed in the first place. "When did she tell you this?"

"Yesterday." Ned leaned back in his chair. "After she had suffered through an interview with Wellington. Who was accompanied by Giles Lawrence, no less."

"Bloody hell," muttered Kane.

Fausto stirred and stretched, leapt down to prowl around the room. Ned added, "Wellington is pursuing some plan of his own. He intends that while he does so, Clea should remain safely at home. He threatened her with my intervention, should she not agree."

Kane wished he might have heard Clea's reaction to *that*. "And yet you let her leave the house."

"The duke," Ned responded blandly, "issued no orders to me. And it would hardly matter if he had. I don't 'let' my sister do anything. The same might be said of my wife."

More was the pity, Kane thought. "Tidcombe told me they've gone out."

"So they have."

"Are you mad?"

The earl considered the question. "Not as far as I can tell. Give me some credit, Kane. The women are well-protected, despite Julie's dislike of being mollycoddled. Moreover, both are armed."

Julie set loose on London equipped with a firearm? Kane felt a familiar throb behind his right eye. "This is your grand plan? Clea is to stick her neck out so far someone will chop it off?"

"Hardly. Julie and Clea have taken Frankie to view the animals at the Exeter Exchange."

Kane bit the inside of his cheek, counted to one hundred. "I thought you planned to keep the brat tucked away until it was safe for her to return to her old life."

"If ever she should want to return, now that she's grown accustomed to a full belly and clean linen." Ned folded Clea's notes, tucked them in a drawer. "As I said, give me some credit. My wife has acquired a page."

Credit, was it? Kane rose, retrieved a decanter from among the volumes on one shelf and a glass from another, filled the glass with whiskey, and drank.

The Exeter Exchange, located on the north side of the Strand, housed on its upper floors a menagerie that at various times included lions, tigers, monkeys, and other exotic specimens — including, currently, a bad-tempered elephant named Chunee — confined in iron cages in small rooms. The roaring of the big cats was often heard in the street below, occasionally scaring horses and unwitting passers-by. Kane hoped Frankie might be snatched up by a tiger. He didn't trust the girl one inch.

He set down his empty glass, turned to find Ned watching him. The earl said, "Why does Clea think you're a prude?"

Kane supposed he should be grateful that he wasn't being called upon to explain how he'd come to be in a brothel with Clea sprawled on his lap. "You don't seem to mind that your sister took chocolate with a courtesan. I do."

"One generally catches less flies with vinegar than honey, but far be it from me to tell you how to best deal with the gentler sex." Ned closed the desk drawer. "Not that you want to catch Clea, of course, but the principle still applies."

But Kane did want to catch Clea; catch her and chain her to his bed and ravish her into a state of satiation so sublime she never wanted to set a foot outside his door.

What would Ned say to that?

Probably that he was mad as a March hare. "I dislike Wellington's involvement in this business," Kane said.

Ned was watching Fausto. Intent on something he alone could see, the cat was inching forward, body low to the ground. " 'Only the dead have seen the end of war'."

Plato again. Kane returned to his chair. "The Bow Street inquiry into Harry Marsden's death has been quashed. By the duke, I suspect."

"Odd, if true. Clea gave me the impression that Wellington was loathe to show his hand."

Fausto gathered his rear legs under him and leapt. A frantic furry creature squeaked and darted away, the cat in close pursuit.

Capture. Release. Recapture. Piles of books tumbled over. The perpetual almanac thudded to the floor.

The library door opened. Tidcombe announced, "The Dowager Countess of Dorset to see you, my lord."

Hannah sailed into the library like a crape-draped frigate. "What are you going to do about your sister?" she demanded, then broke off as Kane politely stood. "Saxe. I did not expect to find you here."

"What can I do for you, cousin?" Ned also rose. "If you've come to speak with Julie, she and Clea have gone out."

"It's you with whom I wish to speak." Without waiting for an invitation, Hannah alit on a heavy oak chair. She cast a pointed glance at Kane. "Privately."

Ned resumed his own seat. "I have no secrets from Kane."

Kane felt vaguely guilty. He certainly had secrets from Ned.

Fausto pounced one last time, caught his quarry by its neck and bit right through its spine.

Hannah shuddered. "*More* vermin? Good Gad!" Fausto snatched up his prize and carried it off to a dark corner. The dowager averted her gaze.

Hannah, it turned out, was not happy about the current rumors concerning Clea's faithlessness and her husband's subsequent suicide. Since the dowager was too mealy-mouthed to state this outright, and since the earl was not in a mood to indulge her, the conversation took a circuitous route.

"As if it is not bad enough that Clea must play ducks-and-drakes with her reputation!" Hannah moaned. "I beg you, send her to the country. Or better yet a convent. At the least, lock her up in chains."

Reminded of his earlier roguish ruminations, Kane winced.

Ned leaned an elbow on the desk. "Why in such a taking, Hannah? This is hardly the first time the gossipmongers have singled Clea out."

"That may be," the dowager said sourly. "But it *is* the first time she has been accused of selling information to the French.

Chapter Thirty-One

How can you hide from what never goes away? —
Heraclites

To the west of Lincoln's Inn Fields, between the Strand and Drury Lane, lay an area called Clare Market, a maze of narrow interconnecting streets lined by butchers' shops and greengrocers' stalls. On Saturday evenings the narrow lanes were jammed with pedestrians and carts and barrows: weary women laden down with baskets and dirty children, aprons filled with produce, and maybe a cabbage tucked under one arm; men smoking, chatting, drinking themselves into a stupor at one or another public house.

The Deacon glanced into the window of a butcher's shop filled with chunks of coarse, dark-colored meat unrecognizable in the smoky flame of a grease lamp. He pushed past a determined doxy haggling over a marginally more appealing slice of bacon in the next stall. The noise of shoppers bargaining for their next night's dinner was enough to give a man a headache, everyone present shouting at the top of his or her lungs.

On one corner stood an old Elizabethan building slightly less derelict than its neighbors. No sign hung outside, this being a private residence and coffee house. The Deacon opened the door and stepped inside, handed his hat to the matronly woman who hastened to greet him. 'Mrs. Russell' was generally believed to be the owner of this place.

Only Mrs. Russell and the Deacon knew that she was not. This knowledge, they kept between themselves. The Deacon walked down the hall into a large room where one man was playing a fiddle while several others engaged in a country dance. Also present were a number of women who on closer inspection, if one cared to inspect them closer, would be revealed as men rigged out in gowns and petticoats and fine laced shoes.

Some wore costumes. A husky milkmaid perched on a patched and perfumed dandy's lap.

The house was furnished in a style appropriate for the purpose it was intended. Four beds were provided in one room, another was fitted up for the 'ladies' dressing chamber. A third room was called the Chapel, where false ceremonies took place. Afterwards the participants withdrew to a conveniently placed double bed, leaving the door ajar for benefit of the spectators, or not, according to their tastes.

The main room was large enough to accommodate much revelry of one nature or another. The flow of spirits was generous, the fire cheerful, the company convivial.

Sometimes the company was more convivial than was prudent, engaging in the sort of behavior enjoyed in Sodom. Everyone knew what had happened to that lot.

This lot, if caught, could expect to be convicted, capitally, of an 'unnatural crime'.

They'd not be caught out here. No privy search-warrant would be issued and put in execution on this house.

The milkmaid removed herself from her admirer's lap and sauntered up to the Deacon. "Pray, sir, how can I serve you?" This said with an obscene gesture and a saucy wink.

"You can't," replied the Deacon. At least, not at the moment. Unless he missed his guess, and the Deacon seldom did, lurking under all that rouge was a Member of the Lower House.

The milkmaid pouted. "Well, aren't *you* a brass-faced bitch."

The man upon whose lap she had so recently been sitting rose hastily, tugged her aside, whispered in her ear. She turned pale, muttered, "No offense intended, I'm sure."

"None taken," lied the Deacon, and exchanged a brief glance with Mother Russell. Come the morrow, a certain pullet would find herself with her eggs all broke.

Abandoning the main room the Deacon walked into another

hallway, climbed the stair. In the upper portion of the house, youths awaited the attentions of the customers below, in the meantime singing bawdy songs, calling each other alternately 'sister' and clever, spiteful epithets, and in general practicing the amatory sportiveness indulged in by strumpets of the more acceptable sex.

Male prostitution was nothing new in London. Trials, however, were much more frequent than a century before. Laws against the practice were known as 'The Blackmailer's Charter', practitioners caught with their breeches unbuttoned generally not caring to face the consequences attendant upon charges. In a certain recent year, more men had been executed for buggery than for murder. The Deacon knocked at a closed door.

"Who is it?" came a voice from inside the room.

"Who are you expecting?" inquired the Deacon. "Lord Liverpool, perhaps?"

The door swung open. Kit Graham glanced uncertainly out into the hall. The Deacon nudged him aside and walked into the room.

Kit was rumpled, unkempt, disheveled. He looked vaguely queasy, like a man who'd stayed too long at Gunter's and overindulged in sweetmeats. The Deacon thought of Clea Marsden, and the debacle in Berkley Square.

"I thought a sojourn here would suit a man of your inclinations," he said. "Have you not enjoyed your stay?"

"I might have enjoyed it more if I'd been given a choice," Kit retorted. "You promised me passage to France."

The Deacon closed the door behind him. Kit Graham wouldn't be the first man to go into exile to avoid prosecution, Napoleon having decriminalized sodomy for reasons known only to himself. Nor would Kit be the last.

Were he privileged to make the trip.

" 'And I looked, and beheld a pale horse; and his name that sat on him was Death, and Hell followed with him'," the Deacon murmured. "Revelation 6:8."

Chapter Thirty-Two

You are your choices. — Seneca

Clea studied her reflection in the oval toilet-glass that rested atop her dressing table. Her curls stuck out in all directions, giving her the appearance of an agitated hedgehog. A hedgehog wrapped in Harry's marvel of a dressing robe, which was made up of cotton in shades of purple and blue, pinkish red and dull yellow in a zig-zag pattern interspersed with multi-lobed lozenges in stripes.

It was a garment far more suited to Pilar than herself.

Pilar, who was no doubt sleeping the sleep of the innocent. Clea put down her hairbrush and walked to the window, pulled back the double curtains and stared out into the night. Reflected in the glass, she saw the room behind her. A silk-upholstered wing chair drawn up in front of the stone fireplace. A walnut cheval fire screen set to one side. Firelight cast shifting shadows on the mahogany wardrobe, the cedar-lined tallboy, the late Tudor bedstead; lent an illusion of life to the fading tapestries that hung on the old wood-paneled walls.

A distant clock struck four.

She let the curtain fall.

Behind her, she heard a slight noise. "Harry?" Clea said aloud.

How foolish. Harry wasn't haunting her. This was what came of being awake in the middle of the night.

Winter in Frenada. A roast goose and plum pudding for Xmas dinner. The officers of the Light Division performing Shakespeare's Henry IV *in a ruined chapel on the outskirts of town. Wellington, at his headquarters, reading a twenty-one point memorandum full of references to dams, redoubts, barriers and signal posts; or alternately blood-stained French dispatches, intercepted by guerillas who brought them into camp. Ordering the flogging of looters, women along with men, six and thirty lashes apiece on their bare rumps.*

Harry had been there, in the background, one of Wellington's trusted aides-de-camp.

Harry would always be there, in the little cemetery where she'd left him, while she went on living her life.

Which seemed monstrous unfair.

Again a faint scrape, this time accompanied by a creak. Clea crossed the room and retrieved the folding pistol from underneath her pillow. She raised it, facing the dressing room door.

Neither ghost nor villain strolled in from the adjoining chamber. Lord Saxe was even more than usually attractive with dirt on his breeches, and cobwebs in his hair.

Clea lowered her pistol. "Kane."

"You were expecting someone else?" he asked her. "Giles Lawrence, for instance?"

Kane had been present, Clea recalled, when she told Giles about the passage in her dressing room that led out into the garden through the old Tudor drains. "If Giles Lawrence came through that door this minute, I'd shoot him. How did you locate the entrance?"

Kane brushed dirt off his sleeve. "With difficulty." A fresh scratch bisected one lean cheek.

His expression was unreadable. Clea was suddenly, intensely aware of him, and her surroundings, and the fact that she was wearing naught but Harry's dressing robe over her thin shift.

Kane eyed the garment, but withheld comment. He walked to the window. "Tell me the brat isn't really masquerading as Julie's page."

"Ned has a theory that the guttersnipe least noticed is the one kept in plain view." Clea sank down in her chair.

Kane turned back to her. "But why the Exeter Exchange?"

"Why not? Frankie wanted to see Chunee the elephant and the 'wonderful Spotted Indian' from Guangaboo. Pilar was curious about the ostrich purported to weigh upward of two hundred pounds. Myself, I was intrigued by the hippopotamus that Byron said resembled Lord

Liverpool in the face." Did Kane look amused? He did not. Clea placed her pistol on the table beside her chair. "Afterward we watched a fire-eater — Julie wasn't impressed, having once witnessed a man swallowing an entire poker — and a puppet show. Later Frankie tossed with a pieman and won. Ned told you that Julie is in a delicate condition? Now that she is emptying her belly with less monotonous regularity, she says, she frequently has an urge to gobble down appalling combinations, in this instance pickled whelks and walnuts and lemonade. Julie and Frankie had a great deal of conversation, about half of which I understood, but they agree that Mr. Pritchett is a deep file — a sly, designing fellow — who would cry rope on his own mother for blood money, in other words a government reward."

Kane was frowning at her. Clea realized she was chattering, and broke off.

She'd known this man nearly all her life. She had no cause to be so ill-at-ease.

Or maybe she did, because he'd kissed her to within an inch of her virtue.

And then dropped her like a hot potato when Mrs. Kingston came into the room.

"You needn't glower at me," she added. "We were perfectly safe. Frankie was disappointed that no one tried to interfere with us. The child has a taste for savagery."

"Frankie is no child. Ned tells me you spoke with Wellington." Kane folded his arms across his chest.

She was not the only one who felt awkward, Clea realized.

One would think that a gentleman with the baron's reputation would be at home in a lady's bedchamber, considering how many ladies' bedchambers he had visited. Perhaps he was afraid she would fling herself at him again.

But then, he was accustomed to females flinging themselves at him.

More likely, Kane was cross because she hadn't taken his advice.

"Wellington doesn't believe Harry shot himself," she told him. "He claims to have been aware of a traitor for some time."

"A traitor whom he'd doubtless like to blame for his own

missteps," Kane snapped.

Lord Saxe, decided Clea, was annoyed with the duke. "I am to remain safely withindoors, Wellington informs me, or at the least to refrain from blundering about and interfering with his schemes. I may take up painting on silk. Or playing the pianoforte."

Kane winced.

He and Ned had suffered through Clea's youthful musical efforts. "Just so," she said. "At any rate, I'm hardly safe withindoors when anyone can wander in from the gardens and set me at odds."

"Do I set you at odds, Clea?" Kane asked softly. He grimaced. "Forget I said that."

Clea doubted that she could. "I shan't apologize. You gave me brandy. If I accosted you, it's your fault."

"*Mea culpa. Mea máxima culpa,*" muttered Kane.

Was he being ironic? Clea chose the path of prudence and let the matter lie. "Wellington warned me that I was not to repeat our conversation. I fear I do not take orders well."

"Either Ned or I could have told him that," Kane said drily. "Had he cared to ask. Ned says you unearthed a notebook. Had you already discovered it, the day I came upon you in the attics? Why didn't you tell me about it then?"

Were Kane's feelings hurt? Clea wondered. And then she wondered why she'd suspected even for a moment that they might have been. "I didn't know what the notebook was."

For that matter, she still didn't. The few coded words Clea had guessed at made no sense. "It's unlikely now that I'll find out. If I had any idea who stole the thing, I'd try and get it back."

Kane clenched his jaw. "Ned tells me I may catch more flies with honey than vinegar. Therefore, I am asking you politely to refrain from taking any more bird-witted risks."

Clea was startled by the harshness of his tone. "This isn't about either Wellington or the notebook, is it?" Or stolen kisses, she added silently. "Just why *are* you here, Kane?"

He met her gaze and held it. "Kit Graham was found tonight, floating face-down in the Thames. His throat had been cut."

Chapter Thirty-Three

It is difficult to suddenly give up a long love. — Catullus

The sun was not yet halfway through its daily journey when Lord Saxe arrived at the Academy. King's Place was largely deserted, its occupants still recovering from the night before. The slumberous setting was not as peaceful as might have been expected. The Queen's partisans were making a great nuisance of themselves, banners flying, music playing, marching four and five abreast, mere blocks away.

A sleepy footman opened the front door. The mistress, he advised the baron, had not yet come downstairs. Disinclined to disturb Lilah in her bedchamber, Kane told the footman to inform her of his presence.

The footman bowed. "Yes, my lord."

Kane climbed the stair.

He had disturbed Clea in *her* bedchamber, in the middle of the night. After all, what was good for the gander was good for the goose. She had already disturbed him in his.

'Disturb' being the operative word.

The house had an air of debauched exhaustion, like a tired streetwalker after her day's business had come at last to an end. Kane entered Lilah's sitting room, left the door ajar.

Exeter Exchange, for the love of heaven. What next, Bullock's Museum?

Soft voices sounded in the hallway. A woman, and a man.

As Kane had pointed out to Clea, eavesdroppers seldom heard good of themselves. Not that he was eavesdropping, and not that he suspected the pair were speaking of himself. Though the words were indistinct, their intimacy was plain.

Kane had never aspired to be the only man to share Lilah's bed. For quite some time, however, he had been the only one permitted to spend the night. Clearly he was no longer so favored, yet another indication — had he needed another indication — that he and his inamorata had come to a fork in the road.

Had Lilah arrived at the same conclusion? Had she meant him to overhear?

The voices fell silent. Footsteps crossed the carpet, moving away. Lilah pushed the door further open and stepped into the room.

Her chestnut hair was loose around her shoulders. She wore only a silk robe. "Good morning, my lord," she said.

Though theirs had once been an alliance of mutual attraction, Kane felt no stirring of emotion at sight of Mrs. Kingston in a state of undress. He could not say when the attraction had begun to pall.

Liar. Of course he could. Once he had touched Clea, he lost all desire to touch anyone else.

Had Kane thought much about what sort of old man he would become, he might have expected to experience a Francis Wakely sort of degeneration into mindless debauchery. He would *not* have anticipated he would grow as weary of profligacy as he was of political maneuverings. "What have you done with the parrot?" he inquired.

Lilah closed the door. "Pepe has been returned to his owner, horizons broadened but overall unharmed."

Kane had not meant to accuse her of cruelty to feathered creatures. "I have been negligent. I apologize."

Lilah shrugged one slim shoulder. "You have had many demands on your time, my lord. It seems the Queen will win her case."

'Win' was not the word Kane would have chosen. So many peers had expressed their conviction of the Queen's guilt, while warning that they would not vote on the Bill if it contained the King's divorce clause (not to mention the perilous consequences of pressing the matter further, due to the present public mood) that three-quarters of the cabinet wished it to be withdrawn. The King was in such an irritable temper that the Archbishop of Canterbury had been sent to calm his mind. "You've heard no more from — or about — the Marsdens?" Kane asked.

Lilah moved toward him, eyes fixed on his scratched cheek. "I have not. I did try to uncover the source of the latest rumors regarding Lady Clea, but with no success."

Her familiar smell surrounded him. Frangipani, heliotrope, musk. Scents that would be forever evocative of Lilah Kingston and her potions and her whores.

Kane stepped back, away from her. She stood motionless, eyes fixed on his face. "What has happened? I am not referring to the Queen's trial."

Kane walked toward the fireplace. He wasn't of a mind to explain hubris to his mistress. "Have you heard who quashed the Bow Street inquiry into Harry Marsden's death?"

"I am hardly in the confidence of the magistrates," Lilah responded wryly. "Though it is entirely possible that a magistrate may have visited my establishment once or twice."

She sat down on the loveseat. Kane said, "I believe you were acquainted with Kit Graham."

"*Were* acquainted with?"

"He was found last night, floating face down in the Thames."

Lilah was silent for a moment. "You are not here to discuss Mr. Graham, I think, or even the Marsdens. If I was a wagering woman, I'd lay odds that you have come to give me my *congé*."

"I would not care for you to remember me unkindly. Pray accept this token of my esteem." Kane reached into his coat pocket, drew out an envelope.

"I am not as mercenary as you may suppose. Your friendship has been gift enough." Even as she spoke, Lilah took the envelope from him. She drew out a sheet of paper, stared first at it and then at him.

In all the time they'd spent together, Kane had never seen Lilah Kingston so surprised.

She had good reason. A royal warrant of appointment was not easily obtained. "The Queen is greatly impressed with the quality of your Magnetic Rock Dew Water," he said, not adding that the Queen was also pleased to, as she had put it, poke a stick in the eye of the old biddies who had avoided her as if she carried plague.

Now that the odds had turned in Caroline's favor, those same biddies were starting to flock around. Mrs. Kingston stood to make a great deal of money from the royal patronage.

Carefully, she folded the paper. "Thank you, my lord."

How formal they had become. Kane crossed the room, paused at the doorway and looked back.

Lilah said softly, "I shall miss you, you know."

Would he miss her? A little bit, perhaps.

Kane stepped out into the hall.

Chapter Thirty-Four

*A woman's reputation is highest when men say little
about her. — Pericles*

The Marquess of Carlyle stood near the doorway of his drawing room, leaning on a silver-tipped cane, greeting his guests. Standing by Lord Carlyle's side, his inamorata was elegant in dramatic black-and-white.

The actress smiled at Clea. " 'Rumor is a pipe blown by surmises, jealousies, conjectures'."

Clea returned her smile. *"Henry IV, part 2."*

Aristocratic to his eyebrows in black evening attire, the marquess took Clea's hand in his and lifted it to his lips.

Lord Carlyle had thrown open his mansion in celebration of his granddaughter's recent return to Town, at the same time making it clear to all present that his granddaughter's husband's sister was under his protection. As Ned had remarked, it occasionally proved advantageous to have an arrogant, opinionated, acid-tongued father-in-law.

Silence fell briefly as Clea entered the drawing room, then the babble of conversation resumed. If none of Lord Carlyle's guests dared snub his granddaughter's husband's sister outright, many slanted sideways looks in her direction, anticipating that the next day's gossip might involve more than the usual 'stuffing the ears of men with false retorts'.

Clea made her way through the throng, listening idly to the inevitable speculation about whether or not the Bill of Pains and

Penalties would pass. The third reading had resulted in a majority of only nine. When Liverpool and Sidmouth informed the King that the Bill was likely to be abandoned, Prinny had threatened to retire to Hanover and leave his ungrateful kingdom to his brother the Duke of York.

As might have been expected, Lord Carlyle's home was the epitome of excellent taste. The walls were hung with pale silk, the gleaming hardwood floors bordered with parquetry, the high ceilings embellished with plaster cornices and intricately carved foliage and glittering crystal chandeliers. Tall windows rested in recessed alcoves, their delicate interior shutters folded back. The doors between the drawing room and the chamber beyond had been thrown open to create a large space.

The air was heavy with the mingled scents of plants and flowers, pomades and perfumes, overheated bodies and candle wax. Clea glimpsed her cousin Hannah, engaged in animated conversation with Lady Georgiana Ashcroft. A prudent distance away, Ned stood smiling down at Julie, who shimmered in a gown of pale yellow satin fastened round her still-slender waist with a gold band. Near the doorway to the music room, Freddy Thompson was speaking earnestly with a plump, moon-faced heiress. Dandy Rossiter — who had bypassed the customary white evening waistcoat in favor of a garment fashioned of crimson satin embroidered with golden butterflies — was observing this courtship through a quizzing glass.

Kit Graham's friends didn't appear grief-stricken by his loss.

Pilar excused herself from the mustachioed military gentleman she had been titillating with tales of Portugal, bustled up to Clea, took her arm. "Smile, *querida*! Recall that you are demonstrating your *indiferença*."

Clea felt far from indifferent. She caught a glimpse of her reflection in one of the many gilt-framed mirrors that graced the walls. Sea green sarcenet with puff sleeves and a narrow skirt— She hardly looked like someone who sold secrets to the French.

Nor did she look like someone who lured rakehells to her bedchamber. Clea was intensely aware of the particular rakehell who was standing near the fireplace at the far end of the large room. What were Kane and Giles Lawrence discussing with such heat? The current political climate. Acquaintance with a certain duke?

Pilar pinched her. *"Não se caçam lebres tocando tambor.* Drumming is not the way to catch a hare. You are staring at *o barão* as if you are a starving dog and he a tasty bone."

Clea said indignantly, "I'm doing nothing of the sort."

Pilar tsk'd. "Do not deny it. I am, as you English have it, 'fly to the time of day'."

Mariel Marsden entered the drawing room, escorted by her son. Her eyes went unerringly to Clea, and her lips drew back in a snarl.

Here was someone, Clea thought, who didn't give a fig for what Lord Carlyle might and might not like.

Amory Marsden moved to speak with Kane. Giles turned away. His gaze passed over Clea to linger on Pilar, who was beyond breath-taking in Brussels lace and richly figured blue gauze worn over white satin, striped silk slippers, and a Turkish turban fringed with gold.

The senhora beckoned. Giles excused himself to his companions and made his way toward them through the throng.

He bowed over Pilar's hand. *"Boa noite.* You are lovely tonight, Senhora Estevez."

"You are very kind, Senhor Lawrence." Had Pilar a fan, she would have fluttered it. Lacking a fan, she batted her eyelashes instead.

A liveried page arrived at her elbow, bearing a glass of lemonade. She said, *"Obrigada, pito."* The page ducked his head and backed away several steps.

Rather, she ducked her head. Frankie, hair cut short and darkened, had undergone a transformation. She was wearing a blue jacket with gilt buttons and a velvet collar, nankeen breeches and, most likely, her first pair of properly fitting shoes.

Giles glanced indifferently at the page, and again more closely. He would be marveling at the presence of the ragamuffin he'd last seen in the attics of Wakely Court.

Clea marveled at it also. In bringing Frankie here tonight, Ned had presented the girl with a purse snatcher's paradise.

She said, in case anyone was eavesdropping, because of course people were eavesdropping, "Julie picked the boy up somewhere during their travels. He needs to be kept exercised."

Frankie scowled.

"Occupied, you mean," Giles murmured. "Why do I think the duke would not approve?"

Clea offered no reply.

Music drifted in from the adjoining room. Violins, with harp and flute accompaniment. Pilar said to Giles, "Such spectacles we saw on our way here! Squibs and bonfires and illuminations. One cannot step foot out of doors without encountering people bearing banners and shouting 'God Save the Queen'."

"The abandonment of the Bill will be seen by the masses as not only Caroline's triumph over the ministry but their own," he replied indifferently. "Soon enough they'll realize it's nothing of the sort."

"You English," Pilar scolded. "Ah, here is General Maxwell. Had I but known— But I did not and consequently I promised that he might escort me down to supper." She awarded Giles a languishing glance over her shoulder as the general drew her triumphantly aside.

Giles's expression, as Pilar turned her back on him, was more than usually sardonic. "All your charm," Clea remarked, "cannot compete with lobster and blancmange and French champagne."

He glanced at her. "You're angry with me. I wish you would not be."

Before Giles could embark upon an explanation of his most recent machinations — *if* he had intended to embark upon an explanation — Mariel Marsden elbowed him aside. In one hand she held a glass of wine.

She glared at Clea. "When I heard you were to be here, I doubted the fidelity of my ears. I don't know how you dare show your face. I pray that my poor Harold never realized you were selling information to the French."

Mariel did not speak softly. Heads turned. Necks craned. Hannah looked as if she wished the floor would open up and swallow her. Pilar clutched her escort's sleeve and pulled him to a halt.

Clea inquired, "What information? That Wellington staved off dysentery by wearing flannel and eating fruit? It was my husband who had the duke's ear, not I. And lest you accuse me again of driving 'poor

Harold' to put an end to his existence, I am not alone in believing he did no such thing. However, I understand that the idea someone else shot Harry is more offensive to you than the idea he shot himself. Members of the better families don't go around getting murdered, after all."

Hannah moaned. Lady Georgiana uncorked her smelling salts. Amory Marsden started toward them. Across the room, Kane scowled.

Clea added, "Nor do they purchase poison to rid themselves of inconvenient daughters-in-law."

"You dare accuse *me*—" Mariel drew back her arm and flung the contents of her wineglass into Clea's face.

Giles stepped forward, but Amory had already reached his mother's side. He grasped her arm, spun her around. "My apologies, Lady Clea. Maman is unwell."

Mariel spat curses as her son escorted her forcibly away.

Giles held out a handkerchief. Pilar, who had abandoned her escort to speed to Clea's side, snatched it from his hand. She blotted the wine from Clea's face and shoulders, dabbed at the liquid that stained the front of her gown. Voices buzzed around them, the gabble-grinders unanimously delighted by this turn of events. Lord Carlyle broke into the babble to observe that whereas society would in general tolerate a great deal, there still existed limits regardless of one's pedigree; and suggested that his guests might repair to the supper room.

Clea saw Hannah hurrying toward them, no doubt prepared to scold her for exposing the family to yet another round of scandal. She said, "I want to go home."

Giles beckoned Frankie, who was hovering. "You, boy. Bring Lady Clea's wrap."

Pilar handed Frankie the wine-sodden handkerchief. "And mine."

Frankie looked rebellious, but managed to curb her tongue.

With all the skill of someone who had vast experience extricating people from potentially troublesome situations, Giles whisked the ladies out of the room and down the stairs. A few words in a footman's ear and within mere moments their carriage arrived at the door.

Frankie skidded up to them, arms filled with fabric. Giles placed Clea's shawl around her shoulders; then, less briskly, adjusted Pilar's lacy mantelet. He escorted them outside, handed them into the waiting coach.

"*Muito grata,*" Pilar said, as he shut the door.

Clea leaned her head back against the seat and closed her eyes.

She thought of Lilah Kingston.

For some sorts of venom, there was no antidote.

Chapter Thirty-Five

Say not always what you know, but always know what you say. — Claudius

Pritchett stood in the private office of the Bow Street magistrates. The room was small and sparsely furnished, the magistrate in residence a heavy-set man with greying hair.

The Runner gestured toward the third occupant of the room, a tall woman of about thirty, thin of person and light of hair, skin pitted with scars from the pox. Her hands were manacled in front of her. She was wearing a dirty apron over her drab dress. "This one destroyed everything. Disposed of the engraving press. Heated the copper plates red-hot and smashed them into pieces. Threw the water-mark wires onto a neighboring dust-heap, where they were subsequently discovered. What I'd like to know is how *she* knew Bow Street was about to pay a call."

The woman thrust out her lower lip. "I didn't know nothing about that. I was just going about me business when you lot broke down me door."

"Burning clothes in the kitchen fire?"

"They was infected with the pox."

The magistrate — Sir John Neville — regarded Pritchett from beneath shaggy brows. "It's your opinion that these forgeries are the work of one man?"

"One man, with several faces," said Crump. "For all his cleverness, our cully won't escape dancing the hempen jig. Nor will his convenient here, unless she stops pitching gammon, her game being truly up."

The prisoner cast Sir John a beseeching glance. "God strike me blind if I know what himself is going on about. It's mace-coves like him as give thief-takers a bad name."

The magistrate shook his head. "It astonishes me how many innocent souls get dragged into Bow Street."

Pritchett shoved his baton under the woman's chin, forcing her face up to his. "You was found to have upon your person a large number of notes, along with a quantity of white tissue-paper that you declared you'd bought to make into air-balloons for your children, which no one with the wit of an oyster would believe. In a situation such as this, a downy doxy would be having a care for her own neck."

She spat, "Mebbe it's yer neck as will be parted from its shoulders if you don't let me go."

Pritchett lowered his baton. "There's penalties, there are, for threatening officers of the law."

She clamped her mouth shut.

Sir John lifted a weary hand. "We'll get no more from her tonight. Take the wench away."

Pritchett grasped the woman's arm, escorted her ungently out of Sir John's office, along a narrow passage to the gaoler's chamber in the building next door.

He saw her settled in a cell. "Cooperate with us," he told her, "and maybe you can avoid catching the hempen fever yourself."

She spat on the floor at his feet.

Pritchett left her to the gaoler. There'd be no bag of bright guineas waiting at the end of this night's work.

Outside, in Bow Street, several of the local residents were merrily burning an effigy of Lord Liverpool. Pritchett nearly tripped over a filthy little mudlark wearing cracked boots and a patched jacket, torn breeches bound up at the waist with twine. "What are *you* doing here?" he asked.

"Said I was to keep me glims peeled, didn't ye?" the mudlark retorted. "I come to report."

Pritchett waved a hand in front of his face, trying to dispel the stink of sewers. "And?"

The mudlark — whose name was Will — allowed he had a

powerful thirst. His pudding-house was empty, what's more.

Pritchett deduced that no information would be forthcoming until these deficiencies were corrected. He took the boy into the tavern across the street and ordered him a drink, which Will golluped up with gusto, along with a meat pastie. When his plate was as unencumbered as the tavern keeper's bald scalp, he let out a stupendous belch, wiped his sleeve across his mouth, and proclaimed himself right as rain.

"I'm glad to hear it," Pritchett said. "And now, a penny for your thoughts."

"A shilling," Will suggested. "And I'll turn into a right jaw-me-dead."

Pritchett produced a shilling. Will made it vanish with all the dexterity of a conjurer with a coin. "Happens you'll like to know as I seen Frankie, togged out like a performing monkey, going into some gentry ken."

Pritchett was less interested in what Frankie had been wearing than the fact that she'd resurfaced. "What gentry ken?"

Will intimated he might like another flesh-and-blood. Once the glass was in his hands — which would have benefitted from several scourings with strong soap — he confided that the house in question belonged to the Marquess of Carlyle, and was located in Grosvenor Square. There'd been some sort of grand occasion underway, nibs and nobs prancing about in their fancy togs. He began rattling off their names.

Listening with only half an ear, Pritchett took another swallow from his glass. He hadn't thought much about Frankie's absence beyond wondering what, while he'd been busy with false banknotes and other fakements, she had got up to on her own.

A canny lass didn't put all her eggs into one basket. Frankie had any number of baskets, each filled with many eggs, her primary preoccupation being the feathering of her nest.

"That dimber mot as popped a collector was there," Will added. "And Lord Saxe."

Pritchett flinched at mention of the baron, whom he was supposed to be keeping abreast of matters, and whom at the same time he'd been doing his damnedest to avoid, a feat not easily accomplished since he'd put himself in a position where Kane knew enough about him to see him convicted for any number of crimes, some of which had been undertaken on the baron's own behalf.

What dimber mot? "Lady Clea, you mean?"

Will nodded. "She left early. Frankie, too. But the jarvey as drove the rattler that left Carlyle House with Lady Clea in it wasn't the same jarvey as was driving when she got there."

Pritchett sat up straighter. "You're sure of that?"

"Sure as I am that water's wet," Will said cheerfully. "And if you was to pass me a yellow boy, I might tell you where they went."

Chapter Thirty-Six

Freedom is a possession of inestimable value. — Cicero

"*Bruto! Bastardo! Chunga!*" Pilar shrieked at the burly thug who dumped her on the damp, dirty floor. The room around them was small and shabby, its ceiling rotting, its walls mildewed. The hearth was filthy with the ashes of countless long dead fires.

A second man lounged in front of the closed door. He was holding a blunderbuss aimed directly at Clea's heart.

Clea had seen that blunderbuss before. First she'd shot its owner in his shoulder, and later in his leg. Regretting that she hadn't put a bullet in some more permanently disabling portion of his anatomy, she said, "Who are you? Not an ordinary highwayman, I think."

"You can call me Toby," he told her. "Not that you'll be calling anyone anything for long."

"*Ações valem mais que palavras.* Actions are worth more than words, *ladrão.*" Pilar climbed to her feet.

The blunderbuss swung toward her. "Give us no more of your jaw," Toby snarled. "Or I'll let Badger here toss your skirt up around your ears." Badger — an ex-pugilist by the looks of him, thick muscles going to fat, flattened nose and mangled ear and fists meaty enough to break a person in half with a single blow — leered.

Pilar placed her own fists on her hips. "*Nunca na vida, porco!*" she spat.

Badger apparently knew enough Portuguese to recognize the word 'pig'. He clamped his hands around Pilar's neck and hoisted her into the air. "Tell your friend to cut the cackle," Toby advised Clea. "Or hers won't be the first neck Badger has cracked."

Pilar was kicking, squirming, and turning an alarming shade of purple. Clea cried, "Put her down!"

Badger lowered Pilar until her feet again touched the floor. She clutched her throat, drew in great gasps of air. Toby gestured with his gun. "Tie her to that chair."

Badger shoved Pilar down onto a nearby wooden chair, pinned her there with one thick hand while with the other he fumbled under her skirt. Pilar kicked him in the jaw.

He grabbed her ankles. She plummeted his back with her fists as he bound her with strips torn from her petticoat. "*Porra! Maldito sâcânâ!*" she shrieked.

"Stop that caterwauling!" Toby demanded.

Badger cuffed Pilar smartly on one ear.

Toby's attention was on the others. Clea fumbled with the strings of her reticule. The wretched things were in a tangle. She tugged at the knot.

His prisoner secured, Badger rose to his feet. Pilar glared but wisely kept her tongue between her teeth. Toby turned back to Clea. "Give Badger your pocketbook."

Clea eyed the blunderbuss. Dare she try and take it from him? Deciding she did not, she held out her reticule.

With one sharp tug, Badger broke the tangled ties. Onto the rickety table that had been drawn up near the hearth, he emptied out the contents of the drawstring purse. Visiting cards, coin purse, handkerchief, Lilah Kingston's antidote—

Toby opened the vial, smelled it, replaced the stopper, tossed it aside. Badger picked up the little folding pistol and tucked it into his coat pocket. Clea looked around the room.

Several chairs were scattered about, and a few other sticks of furniture. A narrow bedstead squatted in one corner. Though the room had no windows, the stink of the common sewer outside still seeped through the walls. Fish oil burning in a clouded lantern contributed to the stench. There was but one means of exit. The splintered wooden door possessed shiny new hinges and lock.

"And so!" Pilar had regained her composure. "Now that you have us, *brigão*, what do you plan to do with us, eh?"

"It's not me as will do with you," Toby told her. "As you'll find out soon enough find out."

"There is a long way from saying to doing." Pilar bared her teeth.

The highwayman's hand tightened on his weapon. Hoping Pilar wasn't going to get herself shot, Clea scooped up her belongings from the table and stuffed them back into her reticule.

The door creaked open. A third man appeared in the doorway. He was fair-haired and clean-shaven, dressed entirely in black save for a simple white neckcloth. For one startled second, Clea thought a clergyman had joined them. Then she saw the pistol in his hand.

A Manton pistol with a large octagon barrel and a silver band inlaid at the breech.

She'd located Harry's missing gun. A chill ran down her spine.

Pilar twisted in her chair to see the doorway better. "*Hola*, Major O'Neil. How curious it is to see you here. It is true what they say, eh? A bad penny always turns up."

"Senhora Estevez." He made her a mocking bow. "Why are you tied to that chair?"

"She booted Badger in the phiz." Toby gripped the blunderbuss so tightly his knuckles turned white. "You told me we was to fetch 'em. You didn't say as we was to treat 'em with kid gloves."

"You misunderstand. I don't care if you toss the senhora out a window," the newcomer remarked.

Clea said, to Pilar, "You know this man?"

"I met Major O'Neill some years ago. He is an even greater *bandido* than Don Miguel." Pilar tugged fruitlessly at her bonds.

"You flatter me, senhora." The major gestured toward the door. Toby and Badger exited as swiftly as if the fabled hounds of hell were snarling at their heels.

"You are fortunate in your friendships, my lady," the major told Clea. "I intended to have this conversation before you left Portugal. However, you were in the good senhora's keeping, which put you under the protection of *O Chefe Guerrilheiro*, whom I did not care at that moment to antagonize, and so I was forced to stay my hand. I did contrive to search your belongings but found only the note I'd sent asking your husband to meet me, which naturally I destroyed."

Clea tried to ignore his pistol. "You shot Harry. Why?"

"He knew too much," said the major "And had guessed even more."

"Needs must go when the devil drives," put in Pilar. "You are behind the various attempts on Clea, Major? And the rumors also? It will have pleased you that Senhora Marsden spread your poison far and wide."

Clea's thoughts were in a whirl, as were her emotions. She was frightened, yes, but at the same time she wanted to grab Harry's gun and blow off this villain's head. "I've seen you before. It was you that slit Clive's throat."

With the hand that didn't grip Harry's pistol, the major pulled another chair up to the table. "Carruthers was a tap-hackled cork-brain who couldn't keep his tongue between his teeth. Do be seated, Lady Clea. I fear we have made a bad start."

Clea sank down on the chair. "A bad start? You murdered Harry. Now you're threatening me with his gun."

Major O'Neill gestured impatiently with the pistol. "I'll have the journal, if you please."

Pilar looked from one of them to the other. "What is this journal? What have you kept from me, *querida?*"

"Journal?" echoed Clea. "If you refer to the notebook I found among Harry's belongings, it was stolen from my brother's house."

The major raised Harry's gun until she was staring straight into its muzzle. "Your husband refused to tell me the journal's location. Don't make the same mistake."

"I've told you the truth!" Clea protested. "I don't know where it is. I discovered the notebook tucked away among various other items Harry brought home with him from the Peninsula. Since he'd never mentioned the thing to me, I didn't know what it was. For that matter, I still don't know what it is. Perhaps you will explain."

"I think that I will not," the major responded. "This is an awkward business. If you truly do know nothing, you are of no use to me."

"*Bom!* At last you realize it!" Pilar exclaimed. "Now you will let us go."

"So that you may run to Bow Street?" the major asked her.

"*Absolutamente não*. When Lady Clea fails to keep several engagements, people will assume she has fled to spare her family further embarrassing revelations, which I promise there will be. As for you—" He looked Pilar over, rather as if she was a filly up for sale at Tattersall's. "Easy enough for a female of your inclinations to be lost in the brothels of the East End."

Pilar curled her lip. "*Via para o diabo!*"

His mouth tightened. "Guard your tongue, senhora, or I will escort you to the infernal regions myself."

The major was intent on Pilar. Clea grasped the strings of her reticule and pulled it into her lap. In that same instant, the door swung open and Badger entered the room.

Tucked under one arm he held a squirming bundle. Blue jacket, nankeen breeches—

"Caught this one snooping around outside." Badger dropped Frankie on the floor at the major's feet.

Chapter Thirty-Seven

The sun also shines on the wicked. — Seneca

Kane was walking down the lower hallway of Lord Carlyle's mansion, preparing to take his leave, when his ear was caught by a commotion at the front door. A young, shrill voice demanded entry. He had a message to deliver to Lord Saxe, the boy said, and no bracket-faced beau-nasties was going to throw a rub in his way. Sounds of scuffle accompanied this pronouncement, followed by a grunt, as if someone had received a kick in the shin. Kane arrived in the foyer in time to see two footmen attempting to send a grubby urchin tumbling arse over teakettle back out into the street.

"Release him," Kane ordered. Reluctantly, the footmen obeyed.

The urchin sidled closer, bringing with him the stink of sweat and sewers. "Grateful to you, guv. And just who might yer nobship be?"

If Kane replied that he was mere John Smith, would this tatterdemalion storm the marquess's drawing room, there to send the ladies swooning and the gentlemen into apoplexies of outrage?

Damned if the idea didn't tempt him. "I am Baron Saxe."

The boy subjected Kane to a shrewd inspection, from the top of his head to the toes of his leather shoes. "A swell of the first stare, swimming in lard. That's what Pritchett said. Himself also said you'd want to come with me. It's about—" He glared at the openly eavesdropping servants. "—a certain dimber mot."

Though Kane had consumed a considerable amount of alcohol in an effort to endure the evening, he wasn't so bottle-head stupid as to blithely set out in company with a malodorous mudlark who likely planned to lure him into some dark corner, there to be set upon by a gang of similarly feral juveniles and have his pockets turned inside out, if not removed from him altogether. Nevertheless—

"*What* dimber mot?" he said.

The urchin's face was freckled, under its numerous layers of grime. "Her name starts with a C."

How many attractive young women did Kane know whose names began with 'C'? One sprang immediately to mind.

"Pritchett warned as you'd be leery," the boy continued. "I'm meant to tell you what I told him." He launched into a colorful account of counterfeit coachmen and dubious destinations and feckless females who in his opinion had more hair than sense. Before he had arrived at the account's conclusion, his tale being at times so embellished with arcane terms as to be nigh-unintelligible, Kane had bundled the brat into his waiting carriage, issued instructions to his coachman, and set out.

Riding to the rescue, as it were. If there was to be a rescue. Kane was more than half convinced he was embarked on a wild goose chase.

He grasped the collar of the brat's filthy jacket. "If you're cutting a sham, you little limb of Satan—"

The boy jerked away. "I ain't telling crammers," he insisted. "And me name is Will."

Kane released him. Apparently fearing no further misuse of his person, Will bounced on the upholstered seat. This was, he confided, his first ride in such a spanking turn-out. He went on to speak for several minutes about beautiful steppers versus bone-setters, his lordship's cattle being, Will pronounced, prime bits of blood and bone.

Kane paid the boy no more attention than he did the streets outside, though the club houses in St. James were brilliantly decorated and all Marlborough was lit up with flambeaux. He heeded neither illuminations nor squibs, window-breakers nor looters, not even a transparency that bore the words: 'May the Queen stand like an oak, and may her enemies fall like leaves'. He was replaying the earlier events at Carlyle House.

The evening had begun unremarkably enough, the marquess having rightly judged the reluctance of his guests to offend someone with so much influence as himself. Kane had taken up a position on the far side of the drawing-room lest proximity to Clea's person cause him to behave yet again like either a hardened lecher or a mooncalf.

Unfortunately, Lord Carlyle's calculations hadn't included Mariel Marsden. For all his influence, the marquess hadn't been able to prevent her making a scene. Even at a prudent distance, Kane had been tempted to behave in a manner unbefitting the gentleman he was supposed to be.

He cursed himself for his lack of foresight. Had he been *less* prudent and consequently closer, Kane could have prevented Clea from setting out for Wakely Court without an adequate escort, a piece of high-handedness that she wouldn't have liked one bit.

She might even have been inspired to wreak havoc on his person. In which case, he might have determined the accuracy of his speculations about what she might be wearing underneath that sea-green gown.

He really was a *débauché*.

Kane rapped his knuckles on the carriage roof. If he *was* riding to Clea's rescue, he was doing so at a snail's pace.

"Crikey!" crowed young Will, as the carriage careened around a corner, pitching a beggar headfirst into his own bonfire. "That was something like."

Impatient, Kane glared out his window — opened to try and offset Will's malodorous presence — at the rotting tenements and taverns of an earlier century, once-fashionable homes that had deteriorated into verminous slums. Narrow, dirty byways teemed with people going about their business, both lawful and not. Suspicious faces glowered as the carriage clattered past.

The streets grew ever narrower, the buildings more decrepit, a confused conglomeration of houses three and four stories tall, their windows stuffed up with rags or patched with paper, their gutters stagnant and choked up with filth. Will pointed to an opening between two dilapidated buildings. "Leave the rattler here."

Again, Kane rapped on the roof. His driver deftly squeezed the carriage into the narrow space, causing Will to comment that it was a rare treat to witness a top sawyer coming coachy in such prime style.

The boy opened the carriage door, hopped out. Kane followed him down onto the broken pavement. The night air reeked of rot and slops and fecal matter. "You might want to look sharp about you," Will advised, as Kane narrowly avoided placing his foot into a pool of stagnant water. "We ain't in Mayfair any more."

So they were not. The night air reeked of rot and slops and fecal matter. Kane would rather have fended off a horde of blood-hungry assassins than find Clea here.

A tall gaunt man wrapped in an ancient brown surtout staggered out of a nearby gin shop, stumbled, sprawled facedown on the cracked cobblestones. "Jug-bitten," Will explained disapprovingly. Howsomever, being as his nibs' satin inexpressibles was shining in the darkness like a beacon in the night and consequently might draw the sort of interest himself would not like—

Will darted out into the street, deftly divested the drunk of his overcoat, and brought it to Kane.

Gingerly, Kane donned the garment, which smelled strongly of fried fish. Leaving his driver to guard the carriage, he skirted the carcass of what might have once been a dog, or cat, or hare, and set out after Will.

There were no streetlamps in this part of town, city officials having little interest in easing the way of the local populace, who at any rate preferred to carry out their various villainous commissions under cover of the dark; no banners proclaiming 'Vindicated Innocence', no demonstrations in favor of the Queen. They passed a woman wrapped in a soiled shawl squabbling with a seller of live squirrels. A man dressed in a greasy shooting jacket buying a pot of foaming beer from a potboy. Ragged sharp-eyed children playing thimblerig.

Around one corner they went, and another, along a passage between two tenements that looked like they might at any moment tumble down. At the alley's end, Pritchett waited in the shadows. He greeted Kane with a nod.

No fool's errand, then. Clea was in danger. Kane drew in a deep, calming breath.

Will gestured to a once-grand timber structure a short way down the street. "The morts was took in there." And a right havey-cavey business it had been, he added, one of the women shrieking like a fishwife, though Will hadn't understood a word she said.

He nudged Pritchett. "There's one of them coves now."

A dark-haired man limped out of the old building, which had a steep time-blackened roof, bulging bay windows and dormers, and great eaves overhanging the ground floor. In one hand he held a bottle, in the other a blunderbuss. He upended the bottle, and drank deep.

Dark hair. A limp. Lest Kane mistook the matter, and he was damned certain that he didn't, the lout had a bruised shoulder as well.

A murderous rage swept over him. Will clutched at his sleeve. "Hold up, guv. You'll queer Pritchett's pitch." Even as he spoke, the Runner was approaching the old house.

The limping man lowered his bottle. "If it ain't the thief-taker. Out for an evening stroll?"

"And a fine evening it is." Pritchett raised his baton and brought it down, hard.

The cur collapsed. Pritchett bashed him with the baton again, and for good measure kicked him in his ribs. Pleased as he was to see Clea's highwayman plummeted into a puddle, Kane wondered what the man had done to inspire the Runner's wrath.

Will didn't protest this time when Kane ventured out into the street, which was now deserted, any pedestrians having prudently slipped away at the first signs of strife. Pritchett grasped one leg, Kane another, and they dragged the unconscious highwayman into the alley. Will snatched up the blunderbuss from the pavement where it had fallen and followed in their wake.

Pritchett lashed the man's feet together, pulled out a set of manacles. Will, watching, put forth his opinion that Pritchett had behaved in an unsporting manner when he crack'd Master Toby's canister.

Kane grasped the boy's collar. "And how is it you know 'Master Toby's' name?"

Will squirmed and kicked, trying to wriggle free. Kane realized he had the brat in so firm a grip he couldn't speak.

He released him. Will rubbed his throat. "Tobe?" came a voice from the street behind them. "Where in bleeding blazes have you got to?"

"That's Badger," hissed Will, and further explained that 'Badger' had enjoyed some success in the ring until the occasion when hard-hitting Ned Painter had beat his nose flat on his face, cracked several of his ribs, and tore his ear half off his head.

Kane peered around the corner, saw a thick-set bruiser standing in the street, holding Toby's bottle and looking confused. Flattened nose, cauliflower ear, heavy muscles turning to fat—

He moved out of the shadows. "Hear Ned Painter gave you a basting. Grassed you neatly. Put you on the Bankruptcy list."

"I can still put out *your* lights, cully." Badger dropped the bottle, the gleam of battle in his eye. While he was prancing and posturing, Kane got in the first hit, a punch to the stomach delivered with great force. He followed it up with a round blow to the left ear, a strategically placed kick to the side of one thick leg, and finally a cross-buttock blow that landed Badger on his back with such force that the ground beneath him shook.

Pritchett emerged from the alleyway. "You didn't tell me his nibs here is a regular out-and-outer," Will said, staring down at Badger, who lay groaning on the ground.

Ignoring this complaint, Pritchett jabbed his baton into Badger's belly. "Where are the females?"

"What females?" Badger groaned. Pritchett smashed the metal head of his baton into the man's jaw.

Badger spat out a broken tooth. "Belowthtairs. In the thellars," he lisped.

"How many men are guarding them?" Kane demanded.

"Thod off. I ain't no thnitch." Badger wiped blood from his chin, attempted to get to his feet.

"What you are is grassed neatly, old slogger." Pritchett lifted his baton again and brought it down on Badger's head. Badger fell back on the pavement, eyes rolled back senseless in his skull. Pritchett produced another set of manacles and bent to snap them on the unconscious man's wrists. "Fetch a constable," he told Will.

The boy darted off, blunderbuss in hand. Too impatient to wait for Pritchett, Kane entered the house.

The place was dark, and smelled of mold. Kane picked up a lighted lantern that had been left by the front door. Acutely aware of having come out without a weapon, gentlemen not being prone to carry firearms to social events, he made his way to the rear of the building, past crumbling walls, doors made of old boards nailed haphazardly together, loose and rotten window frames. At length he came to a doorway that opened onto a flight of stairs leading to the lower floor.

The steps and stair-rails were rotten. Kane proceeded cautiously, hoping he might not fall and break his neck. At the bottom, he paused, listening; then followed voices to a wooden door that stood slightly ajar.

Two strong metal brackets had been drilled into the door frame. Propped against the wall was a stout wooden bar. When the bar was placed in the brackets, the room beyond would become a prison cell.

He heard a slap, a gasp, a thud. Kane pushed open the door. Beyond it lay a small, stifling room. Clea was seated at an ancient table; Pilar, tied tightly to a chair. Frankie was picking herself up from the floor. A man clad in black save for a white neckcloth was holding a large Manton pistol pointed at Kane's forehead.

A parson? Where had they acquired a parson?

"*Quanto mais, melhor.* The more the merrier," sighed Pilar.

Chapter Thirty-Eight

Life, if well lived, is long enough. — Seneca

Clea blinked. Maybe the noxious combination of sewer and fish oil stink had affected her brain. She knew no other way to explain this vision of the usually impeccable Baron Saxe, draped about in a ugly brown overcoat, being held at gunpoint by a man who looked as if he might start quoting scripture at any moment, explaining how the fruits of evil would send them straight to hell.

What Major O'Neill actually said was, "Saxe. I might inquire how you found us, but I fear I'm short on time." His finger tightened on the trigger. "Or, rather, you are."

Clea was visited by an untimely memory of Kane's ungloved hand against her cheek.

And elsewhere.

Hallucination or no, she couldn't sit idly by and see him get shot. Twirling her reticule by its strings, she launched it at the major. Startled, he flung up his hands to protect himself from the missile headed straight at him, its contents flying everywhere.

In almost the same moment, a gunshot rang out. Major O'Neill crumpled, a neat round hole in the center of his forehead, a surprised expression on his face. Clea swung round. Mrs. Kingston stood in the doorway, wearing a severely cut riding habit made of brown woolen broadcloth, holding a brass-barreled pistol in one hand.

"Lilah. Why are you here? Not that it matters. We are in your debt." Kane held his lantern so its light shone on the fallen man's face. "Who was he? Not a parson, I think."

"A true *vilão,* that one," Pilar told him. "By name of Major O'Neill. We crossed paths in the Peninsula."

Mrs. Kingston was remarkably calm, considering that mere seconds past she'd killed a man. "You shot him," Clea stated, sounding foolish even to herself.

Lilah picked up the major's pistol from the floor where it had fallen. "Would you prefer I had let him shoot Kane?"

"Man proposes but God disposes," Pilar remarked. "Would someone untie me, please?"

Lilah looked amused to hear herself referred to as an agent of the Almighty. She nudged the fallen man with the toe of one gleaming boot. "This one is known in certain circles as 'the Deacon'. He has been trying to gain an audience with Lady Clea for some time."

Clea looked from Lilah to the body crumpled on the floor. "Whatever he may call himself, this man murdered Clive Carruthers. And shot Harry, as well. That's Harry's gun you're holding. I would like to have it back."

"It is, is it?" said Lilah. "A souvenir, I'll warrant. O'Neill had far too many irons in the fire."

Kane, who had set down his lantern and knelt beside the major, now rose. "And you know this how?"

Lilah arched an eyebrow.

"*Caracas!*" Pilar muttered in frustration, tugging at her bonds. Skirting the major's corpse, Frankie edged toward her chair.

Did the girl intend to help, or hinder? Clea pushed away from the table and stood up. Kane crossed the room toward her, bringing with him a strong odor of fried fish.

"The major was useful," Lilah added. "But he meant to fling me fairly out of it, and that I cannot allow."

If this was an hallucination, Clea decided, it wasn't one of the sort where the inexplicable was suddenly made clear. "Fling you fairly out of *what*?"

Kane was gazing at his mistress as if seeing her for the first time. "A clever businesswoman knows when to cut her losses," he said.

Pilar rocked her chair closer to the silent Frankie. "We Portuguese have a saying, *pequena. Do mal, o menos.* Of two evils, choose the least."

Lilah glanced in her direction. "You insult me, senhora, if you are calling me the lesser evil. Hallo, young Frankie. You've been as busy as the devil in a high wind."

"Just mindin' me business," Frankie muttered, staring at the floor.

Kane was still watching Lilah. "You put the brat in Ned's house?"

She turned back to him. "Frankie's your thief-taker's pet, not mine. And if she's waiting for Pritchett to rescue her, she shouldn't hold her breath."

Casually, Kane rested his hands on the back of the chair where Clea had recently been sitting. "Major O'Neill. Horus. Cap'n Jack. Each one of them was yours."

Lilah's smile was almost sympathetic. "You are hardly the first to underestimate me, my lord. Do not take it to heart."

Who was Horus? Clea wondered. Cap'n Jack, she knew from Julie's stories, had governed the underworld in the days when her brother's wife roamed the streets much as Frankie did today.

Or Frankie had done, until they locked her in the attics. At the moment, the girl was probably wishing herself still there.

Lilah added, "Ironic, is it not? Baron Saxe's convenient, overseer of a vast criminal enterprise." Her smile vanished as she glanced at Clea. "Which I am now obliged to leave behind. This would not be happening had you drunk your antidote." With one foot, she nudged the vial that had fallen out of Clea's reticule.

Clea gaped at the little bottle. "You gave me *poison*?"

"One never knows when one might encounter a venomous serpent, spider or toad."

Or mistress, Clea thought, appalled.

"Mariel Marsden didn't request that you make her a lethal draught," said Kane. "Nor did she spread those vicious rumors. In God's name, Lilah, *why*?"

"I had hoped the gossip would force Lady Clea to leave town." Lilah scooped up the lantern from the floor where Kane had left it, backed toward the doorway. "Because of her, your ardor cooled, and it tried my civility too high."

Pilar rolled her eyes. "No bitterness burns so bright as that of a woman scorned."

"It's us as will burn," Frankie muttered. "She means to set the house on fire. There'll be no getting out of here once that door is barred."

Not hallucination, but nightmare. Clea cried, "You can't leave us here!"

"*You* underestimate me if you think that." Lilah met Kane's gaze. "Lest you decide our relationship was merely for expediency's sake, my lord, I will tell you it was not. Passion sometimes gets the better of reason, even for a shrewd businesswoman like myself. And now, *adieu.* We shall not meet again."

Kane lifted the chair to fling it at her. In the same instance, she fired Harry's gun, hitting him high in the thigh. He cursed as he fell to the floor. Clea dropped to her knees beside him, tried frantically to stem the flow of blood.

"*Por amor de Deus!*" Pilar struggled so hard against her bonds that her chair tipped over. Lilah moved swiftly toward the open door.

She did not reach it.

Frankie raised Clea's little folding pistol and fired. Twice.

Chapter Thirty-Nine

*It is better to learn from the mistakes of others than that
others should learn from you.* — *Plautus*

It was official. The Bill of Pains and Penalties had been thrown out. The streets swarmed with her supporters meeting, cheering, marching, breaking windows, torching the offices of the London papers that had supported the ministry. A party of Horse Guards was parading in front of Lord Castlereagh's house; the military had been called upon to drive a rampaging mob from the Strand. Another crowd was going about the Aldgate area smashing the windows of any house that was not illuminated in celebration. London glowed with illuminations more extravagant even that those that followed Waterloo.

The Queen was demanding a palace and an increase in her allowance. The King had shut himself away and was having new keys made to his gates.

Some distance from the center of all this excitement, the occupants of Wakely Court were reminded of all this excitement only by the shouts of distant voices and the occasional burst of cannon fire.

A cheerful blazed burned on the library hearth. The current Earl of Dorset was lounging at his desk. His countess leaned against his chair, her attention fixed on Giles Lawrence, who stood near the chimney watching stone maidens and satyrs frolic in the flickering firelight.

Senhora Estevez had seated herself some distance from the merry blaze, not caring — she said — to be reminded that she could recently have been roasted like a spitted pig.

In one hand Pilar held a glass of Madeira, provided by the earl.

Fausto, having recently dined on not one mouse but two, was snoozing, legs extended straight upward, in her lap. The senhora said, accusingly, "You told us you had a plan."

"I told you I was *developing* a plan," the earl amended. "Before it had come to fruition, events took a turn."

"A turn," Pilar echoed. "*Por Dios,* so they did. We are certain that Senhora Kingston is dead?"

Frankie also held a glass. Hers contained not wine but gin, or so the earl had told her, though the taste bore little resemblance to Geneva or Blue Ruin. "Dead as a doornail," she replied.

Idly, Lord Dorset picked up the ugly statue that perched on one corner of his desk. "Who taught you to shoot like that?"

He didn't sound as if he admired her talent. "Pritchett taught me," Frankie said.

"One must applaud his foresight," the earl remarked. "How in the name of all that's holy did you gain possession of Clea's gun?"

"I filched it out of Badger's pocket when he caught me snooping around outside the house."

Pilar said, reproachfully, "You could have cut me loose."

"Cut you loose with what?" Frankie demanded. "It ain't like I had me blade."

Giles awarded her an annoyed glance. "You should have come to me."

Frankie was starting to feel put-upon. "Couldn't very well do that, could I? You told me to keep me eye on her, and so I did."

The earl put down his statue. "Frankie was working for *you?*"

Giles grasped a fireplace poker. "I once numbered among my acquaintances a clever sharper named Earlene. Frankie was her prize pupil, so to speak."

"*É de pequenino que se torce a pepino,*" Pilar observed. "It's when it's small that the cucumber gets warped."

A cucumber, was she? Frankie wandered aimlessly around the room, past stacks of books and various odd objects and maps of the world.

The countess hitched herself up on the edge of her husband's desk. "We've strayed from the point. Frankie here shot Lilah Kingston in her black heart. I don't mean to say she shouldn't have, you understand."

Pilar shuddered. "That madwoman would have burned the house and us with it. Of a certainty, young Frankie should have shot her. I would have done the same myself, had I not been trussed up like a Christmas goose."

Frankie paused by an old globe, gave it an idle spin. "Mrs. Kingston would've wanted to get rid of the makings for those queer flimsies Pritchett was meant to be tracking down."

There was a moment's silence while the others contemplated the implications of this comment. Then the earl sighed. "So many puppets, and Lilah pulling all their strings. It must have amused her no end when I bought that house for her. She already owned half of the West End. And, apparently, certain employees of Bow Street as well."

"In the end, Pritchett bit the hand that fed him," pointed out his wife. "We must thank him for that. Not that we're likely to have the chance. He'll be long on his way out of the country by now."

Pritchett would have suspicioned who was behind the counterfeiting he was supposed to put a stop to, thought Frankie. When a man had several horses in a race, he must at some point decide which he would back to win.

She couldn't blame Pritchett for bolting. Frankie had considered piking off herself. But no sooner had she fired off Lady Clea's pistol than Will had popped up with a brace of constables and his lordship's coach, which had delivered them here to Wakely Court, pulling up at the same time as Lord and Lady Dorset, who'd been fetched home by Giles Lawrence, their own rattler having been filched.

As result of which Will was cooling his heels in the kitchen and probably scheming to steal the silver plate.

Frankie felt the weight of the little folding pistol in her pocket. She didn't plan to return the popper to its previous owner, deeming it fair reward for a job well done.

The earl picked up a biscuit from the plate that rested on his desk and handed it to his wife. "Why was O'Neill called the Deacon?" he asked.

Giles left off poking at the fire. "The major was a younger son, and intended for the clergy. That, combined with his habit of dressing in black— Toby is O'Neill's half-brother, born on the wrong side of the blanket. I should have grasped the identity of Lady Clea's highwayman sooner than I did."

"How amazingly unperspicacious of you," the earl remarked.

Pilar raised one hand. "No more strife tonight, I beg! You knew the major from the Peninsula, Senhor Lawrence, yes?"

He set aside the poker. "I did. O'Neill was present when the Lines of Torres Madras — essentially three strong lines of hillforts commanding the routes to Lisbon — were being built. He was with the Royal Engineers."

The earl opened a desk drawer, withdrew a battered notebook, dropped it on the desk. "Is that Clea's missing journal?" Pilar demanded. "*You* stole it, *querido*?"

Ned smiled at her. "It's hardly stealing when I merely removed the thing from my own house."

His countess brushed biscuit crumbs off her fingers, picked up the little book, flipped through the pages. He added, "I dispatched the journal to Colonel Scoville, who was happy to do something useful. He recently sent it back. Here, Scoville tells us, we have, amid more prosaic accounts and diagrams of hostile encounters, details about a certain corporal's less-than-legitimate activities, including the removal of gold from the Fortress during the sacking of Badajoz, all neatly noted down in Popham's naval code. The journal entries end just prior to the battle of Sanguntum, where said corporal was slain. He had an accomplice, who a short time later was found with his throat slit."

"*What* corporal?" Giles inquired.

"Ask your master," the earl retorted. "Scoville's translations have been passed along to him. It's unlikely we'll discover how O'Neill learned of the gold's theft. Or, for that matter, how Harry came by the notebook and why he kept it tucked away."

"It's doubtful he knew what it was," said Giles. "That notebook contains the location of the gold missing after Badajoz."

"Wellington was attempting to retrieve the gold, hence your involvement," the earl concluded. "But where did Harry come into the business?"

"By accident, most likely. Wellington may have dropped a hint.

When Harry encountered O'Neill in Portugal, they would have got to reminiscing. Somewhere during those reminiscences, O'Neill must have realized Harry had the missing notebook, and Harry must have realized what the notebook was. O'Neill probably thought Harry had also come to Portugal in search of the stolen gold. He would have assumed Harry had the notebook with him, and been furious to discover he did not."

"And a gunshot wound might be construed as accident or suicide, whereas a slit throat would not. What about Carruthers?" inquired Ned.

"During his odyssey through London's gaming hells and brothels, Carruthers became aware of O'Neill's interest in the Marsden family, and said something he shouldn't to someone he shouldn't have. O'Neill silenced him before he could make some equally ill-advised remark to Clea."

"Don't leave for tomorrow what you can do today," murmured Pilar. "Why was Senhor Graham killed? Did he know of this theft?"

"I don't know how he could have," Giles replied. "But Graham was an honorable man who had led Clea into an ambush. Eventually, he would have confessed upon whose orders he took her to Bow Street. As to *why* he did so, O'Neill likely threatened to reveal his intimate knowledge of a certain molly-house."

Pilar stroked a hand over Fausto's plump belly. "This does not explain who searched through my things."

The earl smiled. "Tidcombe doubted your intentions. You having been the mistress of a Portuguese *bandido*."

Pilar sniffed.

Giles replaced the poker in its holder. "The hour grows late. If you will excuse me—"

"By all means," the earl said blandly. "Give the duke our regards."

Giles bowed to the countess, and Pilar. Frankie, he ignored. In the doorway he brushed shoulders with the butler. "The Dowager Countess of Dorset," Tibble announced, and then sped off as if afraid the departing visitor might make off with the silver plate.

Or whatever silver plate Will hadn't yet nabbed, Frankie amended, watching as a black-clad older woman tottered into the room.

The newcomer's irate gaze lingered briefly on Pilar, who had lost her turban at some point during the excitements of the evening, and retained only one striped shoe; then alit on Julie, who was sitting on the desk. "What's this I hear? Clea has been kidnapped? No Dorset has ever been kidnapped. It must be her Fairchild blood."

Lord Dorset had stood up as she entered. "My sister is unharmed. I'm sure you meant to ask."

"I didn't need to ask," the dowager retorted. "If she wasn't in fine fettle, you would hardly be sitting here taking your ease. What have you done with the chit? I must speak with her at once."

"Clea is tending to Kane," the earl explained. "He got himself shot."

"By his bird of paradise," Pilar contributed. "Do not concern yourself, my lady. It is merely a flesh wound."

"Flesh wound, smesh wound." Uninvited, the dowager dropped onto a wooden chair. "You cannot have left them unchaperoned! It simply will not do."

"Are you afraid she'll corrupt his morals?" Lord Dorset looked intrigued.

The old lady blew out an annoyed breath. "Pray don't play the dullard. I am afraid he will corrupt hers."

"What has Kane done to earn such displeasure?" Julie asked her. "Last time I noticed you were among his legion of female admirers, him being such a nicely set up gent. Not to that mention he's as full of juice as Croesus to boot."

Color flooded the dowager's sallow cheeks. "I never!" she said.

Julie plucked the last biscuit from the plate. "I didn't think you had."

Frankie couldn't help herself. She laughed.

The dowager looked as thunderstruck as if the ugly statue had opened its mouth and recited Shakespeare. "Is this the page I've heard about? I shouldn't be surprised that he has no more notion of proper comportment than the rest of you. What use has Julie for a page?"

The earl glanced apologetically at his countess. "My wife is increasing. There are any manner of errands she will need run."

"Increasing!" The old lady pressed both hands to her heart. "Young woman, get down from that desk at once! You must not exert yourself if you are carrying the next earl. We must waste no time in arranging for his place at Eton. The Earls of Dorset have always been educated there."

Julie stayed right where she was. "The Dorsets might go to Eton, but the Fairchilds attend Harrow," the earl demurred.

"Impossible!" cried the dowager. "I cannot countenance such a thing."

"But it isn't up to you, is it?" Pilar inquired sweetly.

"Impertinent!" the old lady huffed.

"Be that as it may," Lord Dorset interrupted, "Frankie saved Clea's life. The least I can do is offer her a place in our household."

"*Her?*" The dowager eyed Frankie's blue jacket and nankeen breeches, both markedly the worse for wear.

"Perhaps as a companion, not a page," the earl continued thoughtfully. "My wife sometimes misses her old life. What do you say, Frankie? Care to abide with us a while?"

The dowager moaned.

Frankie bit her lip. Much as she had enjoyed lolling about in the lap of luxury, did she want to put on skirts and dance attendance on a pregnant gentry mort?

She glanced at Julie. Julie winked.

On the other hand, a girl tucked up snug with a ladyship wasn't so apt to get her neck cricked.

Frankie raised her glass to the countess. "Don't mind if I do."

Chapter Forty

No one is able to flee from love or death. — Syrus

The embers of a dying fire glowed in the bedchamber fireplace. A faded Turkey carpet lent warmth to the old wooden floor.

Baron Saxe lounged, propped up against a mound of pillows, in a great four-post bed. He was wearing one of Ned's nightshirts, his own clothing having been soaked with blood. He was also wearing a bandage wrapped around one thigh.

Kane wondered how many naked male thighs Clea had become intimately acquainted with during her time in the Peninsula.

Her touch had been light, deft, impersonal as she tended to his wound.

She hadn't undressed him. Ned and Tidcombe had done that. Tidcombe had departed with the coat, holding the odiferous garment at arm's length, features screwed up in distaste. Ned had also withdrawn soon after, leaving Clea to play nursemaid.

She was curled up in a carved oak chair drawn near to the bed. Her head rested on a velvet cushion. At her elbow, atop a coffer inlaid with holly and bog oak, a candle burned in a hurricane lamp with a clear glass globe.

Clea stirred, let out a little snore.

Memory served up a vision of a younger Clea, seated in a library chair, reading Ovid's *Art of Love*.

Kane, too, had read Ovid. A long time ago.

Maybe Clea might be persuaded to remind him of all he had forgot.

She said she'd dreamed of kissing him, that night she invaded his rooms. Now here they were, alone again together, and Kane's own current fantasies involved silken cords tied to the posts of this very bed.

He shifted position, and winced.

Clea's eyes flew open. "Are you all right?"

All right? After the evening he'd endured? "Lilah shot me," Kane pointed out.

Clea rose and moved toward him. "As far as Mrs. Kingston's betrayals went, I daresay there were more than thirty pieces of silver involved."

She stood by the bed, looking down at him, a gleam in one green eye. Kane was her prisoner, he realized. Wholly at her mercy. With no hope of escape. As he contemplated the various ways he might like her to misuse his person, she added, "About Mrs. Kingston. Do you mind terribly?"

"I'd prefer she wasn't dead," Kane retorted. "So that I might eviscerate her myself. And yes, I am aware that Lilah chose not to fire a fatal shot. I cannot be overly grateful for it, being as she would have left us to burn alive."

Lilah had tried to poison Clea. He could forgive her shooting him, but he would never forgive that.

Clea sat down on the bed beside him. "I should return to the Albany," Kane said.

She settled herself more comfortably, her back against a bedpost. "You aren't going anywhere."

How would she try and stop him? Kane was no little bit intrigued.

Pilar peered around the door, which had been left ajar. "*Olá!* I am come to be your chaperone. You will be interested to learn Ned has revealed that his countess is *grávida*. Moreover, he has invited Frankie to join his staff. Your cousin is like to succumb to a fever of the brain."

Kane understood the feeling. Clea said, "And Frankie agreed?"

"Of course she agreed." Pilar drifted further into the room, holding Fausto in her arms. "One does not examine the teeth of a gift horse."

Kane was reminded of another guttersnipe, who had invaded Carlyle House with word of Clea's kidnapping and by so doing saved her life.

They'd have to find the boy a place. In Ned's stables, preferably. Kane was much less nonchalant about introducing light-fingered street brats into his household.

Tidcombe's voice sounded in the hallway. Pilar swung around. "What now?"

"Don Miguel Sanchez," Tidcombe announced in sepulchral tones.

A sturdy, swarthy man with long flowing ebony locks and a splendid moustache paused in the doorway, made a pretty bow. "*Boa noite, pessoal!*" he said.

Clea sighed. She might as well try and have her way with Kane in the middle of Berkley Square.

Without waiting to be acknowledged, Don Miguel strode — swaggered — across the room, dropped down on one knee in front of Pilar. "At last, *meu amor!* I have searched for you everywhere."

Pilar tried — though not terribly hard, Clea noted — to disengage her hand from his. "You took your time about it." Her tone was icy. Fausto began to purr.

Don Miguel managed to look simultaneously roguish and repentant. "You mistook what you saw. It wasn't what it seemed. *Tu ès o amor da minha vida.* You are the love of my life."

Pilar pursed her lips. "*Um tigre não consegue mudar as suas riscas.* A tiger cannot change its stripes."

"*Meu coração è teu,*" he protested. "My heart is yours."

"*Falar, falar não enche barriga,*" she retorted. "Fine words butter no parsnips."

He rained kisses on her hands. "Forgive my folly, *doçura.* I swear it will not happen again."

She tilted her head, looked him up and down. "If I do forgive you, and I have not decided that I will, there truly will be no recurrences, you comprehend? Because if there *is* another such occurrence, I will slice off your *bolas* and feed them to the ducks."

"*Assim seja.*" Don Miguel scooped her up in his arms, Fausto and all, and bore her out into the hallway.

Clea couldn't help but smile.

"You were expecting the gallant knight, I take it," Kane remarked.

"The devious *bandido*, you mean. I expected he would make his entrance sooner." Clea contemplated her own gallant knight, about whose person still lingered the faint ghosts of dead fish.

He looked uneasy. Clea wasn't entirely free from apprehension herself. She said, "You will be undertaking no delicate negotiations for Castlereagh until your wound has healed. It is fortunate that this business with the Queen is at an end."

"It has hardly ended. Caroline is determined to attend the coronation. I doubt I need add that the King is equally determined she will not." Kane rested his head against the carved headboard, which depicted an idyllic woodland scene abounding with animal life, including graceful deer and leopards captured in the second before the former was snapped up in the latter's jaws. "I spoke with Amory Marsden after you left Carlyle House. His mother will trouble you no more."

Clea reminded herself to send Mariel Harry's dueling pistols. Thereby putting a period to her association with the Marsden clan.

She crossed the room and locked the door, dropped the key into a blue-and-white glazed Delftware jug. Then she turned and surveyed Kane.

Warily, Kane watched her walk toward him. "I knew that once I kissed you, matters between us would never be the same."

"Do you want matters to remain the same? I don't." Clea reached behind her for the fastenings of her gown, stained now with dirt and water and gore.

He should look away, Kane scolded himself. He should *not* sit here gawping while this particular young woman disrobed.

Was he going to refuse her? Clea watched the muscles clench in Kane's jaw. She tugged at the gown's fastenings. The fabric sagged. She slipped out of the dress, stood before him in her stays and petticoat and chemise.

Kane didn't say a word. Clea was encouraged by the beads of perspiration that popped out on his brow.

She sat on the edge of the bed, her back to him, and kicked off her shoes. "When I understood that O'Neill intended to kill me, do you know what my initial reaction was? I bitterly regretted that I was going to die without having first persuaded you that we should make love."

Clea had never been more beautiful, thought Kane. Candlelight brought out the copper highlights in her mahogany curls; gleamed on the pearly perfection of her body, with its tempting dips and hollows, planes and curves.

She swung round to face him. "You *will* stop thinking of me as a child."

He brushed one smooth cheek with his knuckles. "You are mistaken. I don't think of you as a child."

"I'm glad to hear you say so." Clea reached for her laces, and tossed aside her stays. Her petticoat followed, and then her chemise. Kane caught her wrist before she could strip off her knitted silk stockings; slid his other hand up the length of her leg, from her ankle, past her garter, to her knee; felt her quick intake of breath.

"Ned's nightshirt doesn't suit you." She grasped a handful of the fabric and tugged.

His wound twinged. Kane flinched. Clea froze. "I'm hurting you."

Scruples squirmed, and struggled, and shouted admonitions. Kane said, through gritted teeth, "You'll hurt me more if you stop now."

She grinned.

That grin was his undoing. Kane pulled Clea down on top of him, savoring the sensation of her breasts pressed against his chest. Threaded his fingers through her hair and told her exactly what he wanted her to do to him, his lips against hers as he spoke. Felt her heart speed up, and shivers dance along her spine. He trailed kisses along the fine line of her jaw, down her throat, tasted the pulse beating there; buried his face between her breasts.

She'd never been properly kissed, decided Clea, before she'd been kissed by Kane. His mouth was hot and hard and surprisingly gentle, and sent every rational recollection flying straight out of her head. Including the recollection that he'd been injured. She pressed too hard against him and he groaned.

Clea drew back. Kane caught her before she could remove herself from his person altogether, scooted her forward until she was straddling his hips. It was an obscene position. Clea liked it very much.

She gazed down at the large well-muscled body spread out in front of her. Schoolgirl fantasies held no candle to the reality of Kane. His muscles tensed as she ran her fingers over his torso, everywhere she could touch; trailed her hand down his body, across his abdomen; scooted down and followed the track of her fingers with her mouth. He made a rough sound in his throat, hauled her back up across his body—

And cursed. "Your thigh!" she gasped.

"Forget my thigh." He cupped her calf and tugged her slightly sideways and—

And. He played her, Clea recalled later, like a composer creating a symphony. Emotional minor allegro followed by a slow adagio; lively scherzo with trio; triumphant finale ending with a presto coda and a flurry of sforzandos. Flutes, clarinets, oboes, bassoons and horns. Bass drum, triangle, cymbals. Violins and harpsichord. She soared higher, ever-higher, and Kane was with her every second of the way, until the entire world exploded into a climatic culmination of dizzy, sparkling, cascading notes.

Clea couldn't begin to guess how much time elapsed before her various fragmented pieces managed to put themselves back together, and she opened one eye to find herself sprawled atop Kane amid a tangle of twisted sheets.

She raised up on one elbow to inspect his bandage, which had amazingly remained intact.

He was regarding her with that unreadable expression. " 'When a woman is openly bad she at last is good'," he said.

"Syrus. *Maxims.*"Clea rested her chin on his chest.

Kane smoothed a hand over her curls. He'd just made love to Clea. Or she'd made love to him. What would happen next?

Would she have him?

Did she want him?

She *had* wanted him, demonstrably, but did she still?

He cleared his throat. "Tell me truthfully. Reality did not live up to the fantasy, perhaps?"

This, from the master of musical innovations? Clea adjusted herself more comfortably against his shoulder. "It is too soon to say. I have a great many years' worth of imaginings to work through."

"In that case, I am at your service." His breath stirred her curls.

"I'm pleased to hear it," she said, relieved that he was showing no signs of imminent flight.

Kane waited, but she said no more.

"I *am* a rakehell," he reminded her.

"You're *my* rakehell," she replied.

So he was, and had been from the moment those many years ago when Ned had first sat her in his lap, and she'd examined him with those big green eyes and broke into a delighted grin.

Clea added, softly, "There are many kinds of love, I think. I loved Harry, and I grieved to lose him, but I have been in love with you for most of my life."

She loved him. But Kane had always known she loved him. Why then, was he as overwhelmed as if he'd been given a great gift?

He didn't deserve her. But all the same—

Deserve her or not, he meant to keep her. "I have been experiencing an urge to travel. Perhaps you too would care to leave London for a while?"

Clea's toes twitched with anticipation. "I would like nothing better. Providing you do not intend to visit Portugal or Spain."

"We might go to Egypt. Or India. Scotland might be to your taste. I have a house in Edinburgh. I have not visited it for some time, but the staff—"

Clea ran her hand over his smooth, hard belly. "Kane."

"What?"

" 'The great thing is to know when to speak and when to keep quiet.' "

She could feel him smiling. "Seneca," said Kane.

Epilogue

Whatever begins, also ends. — Seneca

Baron Saxe and Lady Clea enjoyed a long and happy union, involving a great deal of love and laughter, considerable travel, and a total absence of political involvement, to Lord Castlereagh's chagrin and Lord Dorset's gratification, for Ned had foreseen this outcome all along.

Lord and Lady Dorset had the pleasure of a similarly felicitous association, and a fruitful one. Their eldest son did eventually attend Harrow, despite the dowager's protests, as did his younger brothers, although their sister naturally did not. Her father consoled young Miranda that the world was not yet ready for a female Prime Minister, and arranged for her to be tutored at home in every subject that she wished. Giles Lawrence made his own acquaintance with several Prime Ministers, serving Wellington before shifting his allegiance to Earl Grey and William Lamb, then back to Wellington again. Senhora Estevez returned with Don Miguel to Portugal, where they both remained. Though their relationship continued to be volatile, he reached the end of his days with his *bolas* intact.

Harry Marsden, at Lord Wellington's instigation, received a posthumous knighthood in return for unspecified services rendered to the Crown during and after the Peninsular Campaign.

The Queen did attempt to attend her husband's Coronation; when denied entrance, Caroline made such a spectacle of herself that the crowd jeered her when, at last, she drove away. She died less than a month later, of what her doctors pronounced an obstruction of the bowel. The King was not entirely unaffected when he heard the news; after several hours' somber reflection, he consumed goose pie washed down with an abundance of whiskey, sang joyful songs, and ordered that the period of official mourning be kept to the absolute minimum of three weeks.

The gossips whispered that he had finally rid himself of his unwanted spouse.

After the demise of Mrs. Kingston, the London underworld descended into chaos, any number of aspiring villains vying to fill the void she had left; though eventually some enterprising rogues clawed their way to the top of the heap, none ever achieved the arch-villainess status that Lilah had held so long. Frankie and Will both matured into relatively respectable members of society, Will supervising the Dorset stables while Frankie oversaw a school — funded by the countess — where ambitious street waifs were taught rather more useful occupations than peddling produce, or themselves, and sewing a straight seam.

As for the Bow Street Runner Pritchett, he was never seen again.

www.ingramcontent.com/pod-product-compliance
Lightning Source LLC
Chambersburg PA
CBHW022013170626
46808CB00001B/390